Marx Hardy Machiavelli Chesterton Emerson Joyce Austen
Defoe Abbott Melville Montaigne Haggard Cooper Hugo Grimm
Stoker Carroll Christie Maupassant Byron Molière Eliot
Wilde Engels Schiller Smith
Garnett Einstein Fitzgerald Hawthorne Kafka
Goethe Dostoyevsky Hall
Cotton Kipling Doyle Willis
Baum Henry Nietzsche
Leslie Dumas Flaubert Turgenev Balzac
Stockton Vatsyayana Crane
Burroughs Verne
Curtis Tocqueville Gogol Vinci
Homer Widger Tolstoy Whitman Busch
Darwin Thoreau Twain Scott
Potter Freud Zola Plato Harte
Kant Jowett Stevenson Dickens Hesse
Andersen Cervantes Burton
London Descartes Voltaire
Poe Aristotle Wells Cooke
Hale James Hastings
Bunner Shakespeare Irving
Richter Chambers da Shaw
Doré Dante Chekhov Wodehouse Benedict Alcott
Swift Pushkin
Newton

A Gentleman Vagabond and Some Others

Francis Hopkinson Smith

Imprint

This book is part of TREDITION CLASSICS

Author: Francis Hopkinson Smith
Cover design: Buchgut, Berlin – Germany

Publisher: tredition GmbH, Hamburg - Germany
ISBN: 978-3-8424-7718-6

www.tredition.com
www.tredition.de

Copyright:
The content of this book is sourced from the public domain.

The intention of the TREDITION CLASSICS series is to make world literature in the public domain available in printed format. Literary enthusiasts and organizations, such as Project Gutenberg, worldwide have scanned and digitally edited the original texts. tredition has subsequently formatted and redesigned the content into a modern reading layout. Therefore, we cannot guarantee the exact reproduction of the original format of a particular historic edition. Please also note that no modifications have been made to the spelling, therefore it may differ from the orthography used today.

INTRODUCTORY NOTE

There are gentlemen vagabonds and vagabond gentlemen. Here and there one finds a vagabond pure and simple, and once in a lifetime one meets a gentleman simple and pure.

Without premeditated intent or mental bias, I have unconsciously to myself selected some one of these several types, — entangling them in the threads of the stories between these covers.

Each of my readers can group them to suit his own experience.

F.H.S.
NEW YORK,
150 E. 34TH ST.

CONTENTS

A GENTLEMAN VAGABOND

I

I found the major standing in front of Delmonico's, interviewing a large, bare-headed personage in brown cloth spotted with brass buttons. The major was in search of his very particular friend, Mr. John Hardy of Madison Square, and the personage in brown and brass was rather languidly indicating, by a limp and indecisive forefinger, a route through a section of the city which, correctly followed, would have landed the major in the East River.

I knew him by the peculiar slant of his slouch hat, the rosy glow of his face, and the way in which his trousers clung to the curves of his well-developed legs, and ended in a sprawl that half covered his shoes. I recognized, too, a carpet-bag, a ninety-nine-cent affair, an "occasion," with galvanized iron clasps and paper-leather sides,— the kind opened with your thumb.

The major—or, to be more definite, Major Tom Slocomb of Pocomoke—was from one of the lower counties of the Chesapeake. He was supposed to own, as a gift from his dead wife, all that remained unmortgaged of a vast colonial estate on Crab Island in the bay, consisting of several thousand acres of land and water,—mostly water,—a manor house, once painted white, and a number of out-buildings in various stages of dilapidation and decay.

In his early penniless life he had migrated from his more northern native State, settled in the county, and, shortly after his arrival, had married the relict of the late lamented Major John Talbot of Pocomoke. This had been greatly to the surprise of many eminent Pocomokians, who boasted of the purity and antiquity of the Talbot blood, and who could not look on in silence, and see it degraded and diluted by an alliance with a "harf strainer or worse." As one possible Talbot heir put it, "a picayune, low-down corncracker, suh, without blood or breedin'."

The objections were well taken. So far as the ancestry of the Slocomb family was concerned, it was a trifle indefinite. It really could not be traced back farther than the day of the major's arrival at Pocomoke, notwithstanding the major's several claims that his ancestors came over in the Mayflower, that his grandfather fought with General Washington, and that his own early life had been spent on the James River. These statements, to thoughtful Pocomokians, seemed so conflicting and improbable, that his neighbors and acquaintances ascribed them either to that total disregard for salient facts which characterized the major's speech, or to the vagaries of that rich and vivid imagination which had made his conquest of the widow so easy and complete.

Gradually, however, through the influence of his wife, and because of his own unruffled good-humor, the antipathy had worn away. As years sped on, no one, except the proudest and loftiest Pocomokian, would have cared to trace the Slocomb blood farther back than its graft upon the Talbot tree. Neither would the major. In fact, the brief honeymoon of five years left so profound an impression upon his after life, that, to use his own words, his birth and marriage had occurred at the identical moment,—he had never lived until then.

There was no question in the minds of his neighbors as to whether the major maintained his new social position on Crab Island with more than ordinary liberality. Like all new vigorous grafts on an old stock, he not only blossomed out with extraordinary richness, but sucked the sap of the primeval family tree quite dry in the process. In fact, it was universally admitted that could the constant drain of his hospitality have been brought clearly to the attention of the original proprietor of the estate, its draft-power would have raised that distinguished military gentleman out of his grave. "My dear friends," Major Slocomb would say, when, after his wife's death, some new extravagance was commented upon, "I felt I owed the additional slight expenditure to the memory of that queen among women, suh—Major Talbot's widow."

He had espoused, too, with all the ardor of the new settler, the several articles of political faith of his neighbors,—loyalty to the State, belief in the justice and humanity of slavery and the omnipotent rights of man,—white, of course,—and he had, strange to say, fallen into the peculiar pronunciation of his Southern friends, dropping his final *g*'s, and slurring his *r*'s, thus acquiring that soft cadence of speech which makes their dialect so delicious.

As to his title of "Major," no one in or out of the county could tell where it originated. He had belonged to no company of militia, neither had he won his laurels on either side during the war; nor yet had the shifting politics of his State ever honored him with a staff appointment of like grade. When pressed, he would tell you confidentially that he had really inherited the title from his wife, whose first husband, as was well known, had earned and borne that military distinction; adding tenderly, that she had been so long accustomed to the honor that he had continued it after her death simply out of respect to her memory.

But the major was still interviewing Delmonico's flunky, oblivious of everything but the purpose in view, when I touched his shoulder, and extended my hand.

"God bless me! Not you? Well, by gravy! Here, now, colonel, you can tell me where Jack Hardy lives. I've been for half an hour walkin' round this garden lookin' for him. I lost the letter with the number in it, so I came over here to Delmonico's—Jack dines here often, I know, 'cause he told me so. I was at his quarters once myself, but 't was in the night. I am completely bamboozled. Left home yesterday—brought up a couple of thoroughbred dogs that the owner wouldn't trust with anybody but me, and then, too, I wanted to see Jack."

I am not a colonel, of course, but promotions are easy with the major.

"Certainly; Jack lives right opposite. Give me your bag."

He refused, and rattled on, upbraiding me for not coming down to Crab Island last spring with the "boys" when the ducks were flying, punctuating his remarks here and there with his delight at seeing me looking so well, his joy at being near enough to Jack to shake the dear fellow by the hand, and the inexpressible ecstasy of being once more in New York, the centre of fashion and wealth, "with mo' comfo't to the square inch than any other spot on this terrestrial ball."

The "boys" referred to were members of a certain "Ducking Club" situated within rifle-shot of the major's house on the island, of which club Jack Hardy was president. They all delighted in the major's society, really loving him for many qualities known only to his intimates.

Hardy, I knew, was not at home. This, however, never prevented his colored servant, Jefferson, from being always ready at a moment's notice to welcome the unexpected friend. In another instant I had rung Hardy's bell,—third on right,—and Jefferson, in faultless evening attire, was carrying the major's "carpet-bag" to the suite of apartments on the third floor front.

Jefferson needs a word of comment. Although born and bred a slave, he is the product of a newer and higher civilization. There is hardly a trace of the old South left in him,—hardly a mark of the pit of slavery from which he was digged. His speech is as faultless as his dress. He is clean, close-shaven, immaculate, well-groomed, silent,—reminding me always of a mahogany-colored Greek professor, even to his eye-glasses. He keeps his rooms in admirable order, and his household accounts with absolute accuracy; never spilled a drop of claret, mixed a warm cocktail, or served a cold plate in his life; is devoted to Hardy, and so punctiliously polite to his master's friends and guests that it is a pleasure to have him serve you.

Strange to say, this punctilious politeness had never extended to the major, and since an occurrence connected with this very bag, to be related shortly, it had ceased altogether. Whether it was that Jefferson had always seen through the peculiar varnish that made bright the major's veneer, or whether in an unguarded moment, on a previous visit, the major gave way to some such outburst as he would have inflicted upon the domestics of his own establishment, forgetting for the time the superior position to which Jefferson's breeding and education entitled him, I cannot say, but certain it is that while to all outward appearances Jefferson served the major with every indication of attention and humility, I could see under it all a quiet reserve which marked the line of unqualified disapproval. This was evident even in the way he carried the major's bag,— holding it out by the straps, not as became the handling of a receptacle containing a gentleman's wardrobe, but by the neck, so to speak,—as a dog to be dropped in the gutter.

It was this bag, or rather its contents, or to be more exact its lack of contents, that dulled the fine edge of Jefferson's politeness. He unpacked it, of course, with the same perfunctory care that he would have bestowed on the contents of a Bond Street Gladstone, indulging in a prolonged chuckle when he found no trace of a most important part of a gentleman's wardrobe,—none of any pattern. It was, therefore, with a certain grim humor that, when he showed the major to his room the night of his arrival, he led gradually up to a question which the unpacking a few hours before had rendered inevitable.

"Mr. Hardy's orders are that I should inform every gentleman when he retires that there's plenty of whiskey and cigars on the sideboard, and that"—here Jefferson glanced at the bag—"and that if any gentleman came unprepared there was a night shirt and a pair of pajams in the closet."

"I never wore one of 'em in my life, Jefferson; but you can put the whiskey and the cigars on the chair by my bed, in case I wake in the night."

When Jefferson, in answer to my inquiries as to how the major had passed the night, related this incident to me the following morning, I could detect, under all his deference and respect toward his master's guest, a certain manner and air plainly implying that, so far as the major and himself were concerned, every other but the most diplomatic of relations had been suspended.

The major, by this time, was in full possession of my friend's home. The only change in his dress was in the appearance of his shoes, polished by Jefferson to a point verging on patent leather, and the adoption of a black alpaca coat, which, although it wrinkled at the seams with a certain home-made air, still fitted his fat shoulders very well. To this were added a fresh shirt and collar, a white tie, nankeen vest, and the same tight-fitting, splay-footed trousers, enriched by a crease of Jefferson's own making.

As he lay sprawled out on Hardy's divan, with his round, rosy, clean-shaven face, good-humored mouth, and white teeth, the whole enlivened by a pair of twinkling eyes, you forgot for the moment that he was not really the sole owner of the establishment. Further intercourse thoroughly convinced you of a similar lapse of memory on the major's part.

"My dear colonel, let me welcome you to my New York home!" he exclaimed, without rising from the divan. "Draw up a chair; have a mouthful of mocha? Jefferson makes it delicious. Or shall I call him to broil another po'ter-house steak? No? Then let me ring for some cigars," and he touched the bell.

To lie on a divan, reach out one arm, and, with the expenditure of less energy than would open a match-box, to press a button summoning an attendant with all the unlimited comforts of life, — juleps, cigars, coffee, cocktails, morning papers, fans, matches out of arm's reach, everything that soul could covet and heart long for; to see all these several commodities and luxuries develop, take shape, and materialize while he lay flat on his back, — this to the major was civilization.

"But, colonel, befo' you sit down, fling yo' eye over that garden in the square. Nature in her springtime, suh!"

I agreed with the major, and was about to take in the view over the treetops, when he tucked another cushion under his head, elongated his left leg until it reached the window-sill, thus completely monopolizing it,-and continued without drawing a breath: —

"And I am so comfo'table here. I had a po'ter-house steak this mornin'—you're sure you won't have one?" I shook my head. "A po'ter-house steak, suh, that'll haunt my memory for days. We, of co'se, have at home every variety of fish, plenty of soft-shell crabs, and 'casionally a canvasback, when Hardy or some of my friends are lucky enough to hit one, but no meat that is wo'th the cookin'. By the bye, I've come to take Jack home with me; the early strawberries are in their prime, now. You will join us, of course?"

Before I could reply, Jefferson entered the room, laid a tray of cigars and cigarettes with a small silver alcohol lamp at my elbow, and, with a certain inquiring and, I thought, slightly surprised glance at the major's sprawling attitude, noiselessly withdrew. The major must have caught the expression on Jefferson's face, for he dropped his telescope leg, and straightened up his back, with the sudden awkward movement of a similarly placed lounger surprised by a lady in a hotel parlor. The episode seemed to knock the enthusiasm out of him, for after a moment he exclaimed in rather a subdued tone: —

"Rather remarkable nigger, this servant of Jack's. I s'pose it is the influence of yo' New York ways, but I am not accustomed to his kind."

I began to defend Jefferson, but he raised both hands in protest.

"Yes, I know—education and thirty dollars a month. All very fine, but give me the old house-servants of the South—the old Anthonys, and Keziahs, and Rachels. They never went about rigged up like a stick of black sealing-wax in a suit of black co't-plaster. They were easy-goin' and comfortable. Yo' interest was their interest; they bore yo' name, looked after yo' children, and could look after yo' house, too. Now see this nigger of Jack's; he's better dressed than I am, tips round as solemn on his toes as a marsh-crane, and yet I'll bet a dollar he's as slick and cold-hearted as a high-water clam. That's what education has done for *him*.

"You never knew Anthony, my old butler? Well, I want to tell you, he *was* a servant, as *was* a servant. During Mrs. Slocomb's life"—here the major assumed a reminiscent air, pinching his fat chin with his thumb and forefinger—"we had, of co'se, a lot of niggers; but this man Anthony! By gravy! when he filled yo' glass with some of the old madeira that had rusted away in my cellar for half a century,"—here the major now slipped his thumb into the armhole of his vest,—"it tasted like the nectar of the gods, just from the way Anthony poured it out.

"But you ought to have seen him move round the table when dinner was over! He'd draw himself up like a drum-major, and throw back the mahogany doors for the ladies to retire, with an air that was captivatin'." The major was now on his feet—his reminiscent mood was one of his best. "That's been a good many years ago, colonel, but I can see him now just as plain as if he stood before me, with his white cotton gloves, white vest, and green coat with brass buttons, standin' behind Mrs. Slocomb's chair. I can see the old sidebo'd, suh, covered with George III. silver, heirlooms of a century,"—this with a trance-like movement of his hand across his eyes. "I can see the great Italian marble mantels suppo'ted on lions' heads, the inlaid floor and wainscotin'."—Here the major sank upon the divan again, shutting both eyes reverently, as if these memories of the past were a sort of religion with him.

"And the way those niggers loved us! And the many holes they helped us out of. Sit down there, and let me tell you what Anthony did for me once." I obeyed cheerfully. "Some years ago I received a telegram from a very intimate friend of mine, a distinguished Baltimorean, — the Nestor of the Maryland bar, suh, — informin' me that he was on his way South, and that he would make my house his home on the foll]owin' night." The major's eyes were still shut. He had passed out of his reverential mood, but the effort to be absolutely exact demanded concentration.

"I immediately called up Anthony, and told him that Judge Spofford of the Supreme Co't of Maryland would arrive the next day, and that I wanted the best dinner that could be served in the county, and the best bottle of wine in my cellar." The facts having been correctly stated, the major assumed his normal facial expression and opened his eyes.

"What I'm tellin' you occurred after the war, remember, when putty near everybody down our way was busted. Most of our niggers had run away, — all 'cept our old house-servants, who never forgot our family pride and our noble struggle to keep up appearances. Well, suh, when Spofford arrived Anthony carried his bag to his room, and when dinner was announced, if it *was* my own table, I must say that it cert'ly did fa'rly groan with the delicacies of the season. After the crabs had been taken off, — we were alone, Mrs. Slocomb havin' gone to Baltimo', — I said to the judge: 'Yo' Honor, I am now about to delight yo' palate with the very best bottle of old madeira that ever passed yo' lips. A wine that will warm yo' heart, and unbutton the top button of yo' vest. It is part of a special importation presented to Mrs. Slocomb's father by the captain of one of his ships. — Anthony, go down into the wine-cellar, the inner cellar, Anthony, and bring me a bottle of that old madeira of '37 — stop, Anthony; make it '39. I think, judge, it is a little dryer.' Well, Anthony bowed, and left the room, and in a few moments he came back, set a lighted candle on the mantel, and, leanin' over my chair, said in a loud whisper: 'De cellar am locked, suh, and I'm 'feard Mis' Slocomb dun tuk de key.'

"'Well, s'pose she has,' I said; 'put yo' knee against it, and fo'ce the do'.' I knew my man, suh. Anthony never moved a muscle.

"Here the judge called out, 'Why, major, I couldn't think of'—

"'Now, yo' Honor,' said I, 'please don't say a word. This is my affair. The lock is not of the slightest consequence.'

"In a few minutes back comes Anthony, solemn as an owl. 'Major,' said he, 'I done did all I c'u'd, an' dere ain't no way 'cept breakin' down de do'. Las' time I done dat, Mis' Slocomb neber forgib me fer a week.'

"The judge jumped up. 'Major, I won't have you breakin' yo' locks and annoyin' Mrs. Slocomb.'

"'Yo' Honor,' I said, 'please take yo' seat. I'm d——d if you shan't taste that wine, if I have to blow out the cellar walls.'

"'I tell you, major,' replied the judge in a very emphatic tone and with some slight anger I thought, 'I ought not to drink yo' high-flavored madeira; my doctor told me only last week I must stop that kind of thing. If yo' servant will go upstairs and get a bottle of whiskey out of my bag, it's just what I ought to drink.'

"Now I want to tell you, colonel, that at that time I hadn't had a bottle of any kind of wine in my cellar for five years." Here the major closed one eye, and laid his forefinger against his nose.

"'Of co'se, yo' Honor,' I said, 'when you put it on a matter of yo' health I am helpless; that paralyzes my hospitality; I have not a word to say. Anthony, go upstairs and get the bottle.' And we drank the judge's whiskey! Now see the devotion and loyalty of that old negro servant, see his shrewdness! Do you think this marsh-crane of Jack's"—

Here Jefferson threw open the door, ushering in half a dozen gentlemen, and among them the rightful host, just returned after a week's absence,—cutting off the major's outburst, and producing another equally explosive:—

"Why, Jack!"

Before the two men grasp hands I must, in all justice to the major, say that he not only had a sincere admiration for Jack's surroundings, but also for Jack himself, and that while he had not the slightest compunction in sharing or, for that matter, monopolizing his hospitality, he would have been equally generous in return had it been possible for him to revive the old days, and to afford a menage equally lavish.

It is needless for me to make a like statement for Jack. One half the major's age, trained to practical business life from boyhood, frank, spontaneous, every inch a man, kindly natured, and, for one so young, a deep student, of men as well as of books, it was not to be wondered at that not only the major but that every one else who knew him loved him. The major really interested him enormously. He represented a type which was new to him, and which it delighted him to study. The major's heartiness, his magnificent disregard for *meum* and *tuum*, his unique and picturesque mendacity, his grandiloquent manners at times, studied, as he knew, from some example of the old regime, whom he either consciously or unconsciously imitated, his peculiar devotion to the memory of his late wife,—all appealed to Jack's sense of humor, and to his enjoyment of anything out of the common. Under all this he saw, too, away down in the major's heart, beneath these several layers, a substratum of true kindness and tenderness.

This kindness, I know, pleased Jack best of all.

So when the major sprang up in delight, calling out, "Why, Jack!" it was with very genuine, although quite opposite individual, sympathies, that the two men shook hands. It was beautiful, too, to see the major welcome Jack to his own apartments, dragging up the most comfortable chair in the room, forcing him into it, and tucking a cushion under his head, or ringing up Jefferson every few moments for some new luxury. These he would catch away from that perfectly trained servant's tray, serving them himself, rattling on all the time as to how sorry he was that he did not know the exact hour at which Jack would arrive, that he might have had breakfast on the table—how hot had it been on the road—how well he was looking, etc.

It was specially interesting, besides, after the proper introductions had been made, to note the way in which Jack's friends, inoculated with the contagion of the major's mood, and carried away by his breezy, buoyant enthusiasm, encouraged the major to flow on, interjecting little asides about his horses and farm stock, agreeing to a man that the two-year old colt—a pure creation on the moment of the major—would certainly beat the record and make the major's fortune, and inquiring with great solicitude whether the major felt quite sure that the addition to the stables which he contemplated would be large enough to accommodate his stud, with other similar inquiries which, while indefinite and tentative, were, so to speak, but flies thrown out on the stream of talk,—the major rising continuously, seizing the bait, and rushing headlong over sunken rocks and through tangled weeds of the improbable in a way that would have done credit to a Munchausen of older date. As for Jack, he let him run on. One plank in the platform of his hospitality was to give every guest a free rein.

Before the men separated for the day, the major had invited each individual person to make Crab Island his home for the balance of his life, regretting that no woman now graced his table since Mrs. Slocomb's death,—"Major Talbot's widow—Major John Talbot of Pocomoke, suh," this impressively and with sudden gravity of tone,—placing his stables, his cellar, and his servants at their disposal, and arranging for everybody to meet everybody else the following day in Baltimore, the major starting that night, and Jack and his friends the next day. The whole party would then take passage on board one of the Chesapeake Bay boats, arriving off Crab Island at daylight the succeeding morning.

This was said with a spring and joyousness of manner, and a certain quickness of movement, that would surprise those unfamiliar with some of the peculiarities of Widow Talbot's second husband. For with that true spirit of vagabondage which saturated him, next to the exquisite luxury of lying sprawled on a lounge with a noiseless servant attached to the other end of an electric wire, nothing delighted the major so much as an outing, and no member of any such junketing party, be it said, was more popular every hour of the journey. He could be host, servant, cook, chambermaid, errand-boy, and *grand seigneur* again in the same hour, adapting himself to every emergency that arose. His good-humor was perennial, unceasing, one constant flow, and never checked. He took care of the dogs, unpacked the bags, laid out everybody's linen, saw that the sheets were dry, received all callers so that the boys might sleep in the afternoon, did all the disagreeable and uncomfortable things himself, and let everybody else have all the fun. He did all this unconsciously, graciously, and simply because he could not help it. When the outing ended, you parted from him with all the regret that you would from some chum of your college days. As for him, he never wanted it to end. There was no office, nor law case, nor sick patient, nor ugly partner, nor complication of any kind, commercial, social, or professional, which could affect the major. For him life was one prolonged drift: so long as the last man remained he could stay. When he left, if there was enough in the larder to last over, the major always made another day of it.

II

The major was standing on the steamboat wharf in Baltimore, nervously consulting his watch, when Jack and I stepped from a cab next day.

"Well, by gravy! is this all? Where are the other gentlemen?"

"They'll be down in the morning, major," said Jack. "Where shall we send this baggage?"

"Here, just give it to me! Po'ter, *po'ter*!" in a stentorian voice. "Take these bags and guns, and put 'em on the upper deck alongside of my luggage. Now, gentlemen, just a sip of somethin' befo' they haul the gang-plank,—we've six minutes yet."

The bar was across the street. On the way over, the major confided to Jack full information regarding the state-rooms, remarking that he had selected the "fo' best on the upper deck," and adding that he would have paid for them himself only a friend had disappointed him.

It was evident that the barkeeper knew his peculiarities, for a tall, black bottle with a wabbly cork—consisting of a porcelain marble confined in a miniature bird-cage—was passed to the major before he had opened his mouth. When he did open it—the mouth—there was no audible protest as regards the selection. When he closed it again the flow line had fallen some three fingers. It is, however, fair to the major to say that only one third of this amount was tucked away under his own waistcoat.

The trip down the bay was particularly enjoyable, brightened outside on the water by the most brilliant of sunsets, the afternoon sky a glory of purple and gold, and made gay and delightful inside the after-cabin by the charm of the major's talk,—the whole passenger-list entranced as he skipped from politics and the fine arts to literature, tarrying a moment in his flight to discuss a yellow-backed book that had just been published, and coming to a full stop with the remark:—

"And you haven't read that book, Jack,—that scurrilous attack on the industries of the South? My dear fellow! I'm astounded that a man of yo' gifts should not—Here—just do me the favor to look through my baggage on the upper deck, and bring me a couple of books lyin' on top of my dressin'-case."

"Which trunk, major?" asked Jack, a slight smile playing around his mouth.

"Why, my sole-leather trunk, of co'se; or perhaps that English hat-box—no, stop, Jack, come to think, it is in the small valise. Here, take my keys," said the major, straightening his back, squeezing his fat hand into the pocket of his skin-tight trousers, and fishing up with his fore-finger a small bunch of keys. "Right on top, Jack; you can't miss it."

"Isn't he just too lovely for anything?" said Jack to me, when we reached the upper deck,—I had followed him out. "He's wearing now the only decent suit of clothes he owns, and the rest of his wardrobe you could stuff into a bandbox. English sole-leather trunk! Here, put your thumb on that catch," and he drew out the major's bag,—the one, of course, that Jefferson unpacked, with the galvanized-iron clasps and paper-leather sides.

The bag seemed more rotund, and heavier, and more important looking than when I handled it that afternoon in front of Delmonico's, presenting a well-fed, even a bloated, appearance. The clasps, too, appeared to have all they could do to keep its mouth shut, while the hinges bulged in an ominous way.

I started one clasp, the other gave way with a burst, and the next instant, to my horror, the major's wardrobe littered the deck. First the books, then a package of tobacco, then the one shirt, porcelain-finished collars, and the other necessaries, including a pair of slip-pers and a comb. Next, three bundles loosely wrapped, one containing two wax dolls, the others some small toys, and a cheap Noah's ark, and last of all, wrapped up in coarse, yellow butcher's paper, stained and moist, a freshly cut porter-house steak.

Jack roared with laughter as he replaced the contents. "Yes; toys for the little children—he never goes back without something for them if it takes his last dollar; tobacco for his old cook, Rachel; not a thing for himself, you see—and this steak! Who do you suppose he bought that for?"

"Did you find it?" called out the major, as we reëntered the cabin.

"Yes; but it wasn't in the English trunk," said Jack, handing back the keys, grave as a judge, not a smile on his face.

"Of co'se not; didn't I tell you it was in the small bag? Now, gentlemen, listen!" turning the leaves. "Here is a man who has the impertinence to say that our industries are paralyzed. It is not our industries; it is our people. Robbed of their patrimony, their fields laid waste, their estates confiscated by a system of foreclosure lackin' every vestige of decency and co'tesy,—Shylocks wantin' their pound of flesh on the very hour and day,—why shouldn't they be paralyzed?" He laughed heartily. "Jack, you know Colonel Dorsey Kent, don't you?"

Jack did not, but the owners of several names on the passenger-list did, and hitched their camp-stools closer.

"Well, Kent was the only man I ever knew who ever held out against the damnable oligarchy."

Here an old fellow in a butternut suit, with a half-moon of white whiskers tied under his chin, leaned forward in rapt attention.

The major braced himself, and continued: "Kent, gentlemen, as many of you know, lived with his maiden sister over on Tinker Neck, on the same piece of ground where he was bo'n. She had a life interest in the house and property, and it was so nominated in the bond. Well, when it got down to hog and hominy, and very little of that, she told Kent she was goin' to let the place to a strawberry-planter from Philadelphia, and go to Baltimo' to teach school. She was sorry to break up the home, but there was nothin' else to do.

Well, it hurt Kent to think she had to leave home and work for her living, for he was a very tender-hearted man.

"'You don't say so, Jane,' said he, 'and you raised here! Isn't that very sudden?' She told him it was, and asked him what he was going to do for a home when the place was rented?

"'Me, Jane? I shan't do anythin'. I shall stay here. If your money affairs are so badly mixed up that you're obliged to leave yo' home, I am very deeply grieved, but I am powerless to help. I am not responsible for the way this war ended. I was born here, and here I am going to stay." And he did. Nothing could move him. She finally had to rent him with the house,—he to have three meals a day, and a room over the kitchen.

"For two years after that Kent was so disgusted with life, and the turn of events, that he used to lie out on a rawhide, under a big sycamore tree in front of the po'ch, and get a farm nigger to pull him round into the shade by the tail of the hide, till the grass was wore as bare as yo' hand. Then he got a bias-cut rockin'-chair, and rocked himself round.

"The strawberry man said, of co'se, that he was too lazy to live. But I look deeper than that. To me, gentlemen, it was a crushin', silent protest against the money power of our times. And it never broke his spirit, neither. Why, when the census man came down a year befo' the colonel's death, he found him sittin' in his rockin'-chair, bare-headed. Without havin' the decency to take off his own hat, or even ask Kent's permission to speak to him, the census man began askin' questions,—all kinds, as those damnable fellows do. Colonel Kent let him ramble on for a while, then he brought him up standin'.

"'Who did you say you were, suh?'

"'The United States census-taker.'

"'Ah, a message from the enemy. Take a seat on the grass.'

"'It's only a matter of form,' said the man.

"'So I presume, and very bad form, suh,' looking at the hat still on the man's head. 'But go on.'

"'Well, what's yo' business?' asked the agent, taking out his book and pencil.

"'My business, suh?' said the colonel, risin' from his chair, mad clear through, — 'I've no business, suh. I am a prisoner of war waitin' to be exchanged!' and he stomped into the house."

Here the major burst into a laugh, straightened himself up to his full height, squeezed the keys back into his pocket, and said he must take a look into the state-rooms on the deck to see if they were all ready for his friends for the night.

When I turned in for the night, he was on deck again, still talking, his hearty laugh ringing out every few moments. Only the white-whiskered man was left. The other camp-stools were empty.

II

At early dawn the steamboat slowed down, and a scow, manned by two bare-footed negroes with sweep oars, rounded to. In a few moments the major, two guns, two valises, Jack, and I were safely landed on its wet bottom, the major's bag with its precious contents stowed between his knees.

To the left, a mile or more away, lay Crab Island, the landed estate of our host, — a delicate, green thread on the horizon line, broken by two knots, one evidently a large house with chimneys, and the other a clump of trees. The larger knot proved to be the manor house that sheltered the belongings of the major, with the wine-cellars of marvelous vintage, the table that groaned, the folding mahogany doors that swung back for bevies of beauties, and perhaps, for all I knew, the gray-haired, ebony butler in the green coat. The smaller knot, Jack said, screened from public view the little club-house belonging to his friends and himself.

As the sun rose and we neared the shore, there came into view on the near end of the island the rickety outline of a palsied old dock, clutching with one arm a group of piles anchored in the marsh grass, and extending the other as if in welcome to the slow-moving scow. We accepted the invitation, threw a line over a thumb of a pile, and in five minutes were seated in a country stage. Ten more, and we backed up to an old-fashioned colonial porch, with sloping roof and dormer windows supported by high white columns. Leaning over the broken railing of the porch was a half-grown negro boy, hatless and bare-footed; inside the door, looking furtively out, half concealing her face with her apron, stood an old negro woman, her head bound with a bandana kerchief, while peeping from behind an outbuilding was a group of children in sun-bonnets and straw hats,—"the farmer's boys and girls," the major said, waving his hand, as we drove up, his eyes brightening. Then there was the usual collection of farm-yard fowl, beside two great hounds, who visited each one of us in turn, their noses rubbing our knees.

If the major, now that he was on his native heath, realized in his own mind any difference between the Eldorado which his eloquence had conjured up in my own mind, the morning before in Jack's room, and the hard, cold facts before us, he gave no outward sign. To all appearances, judging from his perfect ease and good temper, the paint-scaled pillars were the finest of Carrara marble, the bare floors were carpeted with the softest fabrics of Turkish looms, and the big, sparsely furnished rooms were so many salons, where princes trod in pride, and fair ladies stepped a measure.

The only remark he made was in answer to a look of surprise on my face when I peered curiously into the bare hall and made a cursory mental inventory of its contents.

"Yes, colonel; you will find, I regret to say, some slight changes since the old days. Then, too, my home is in slight confusion owin' to the spring cleanin', and a good many things have been put away."

I looked to Jack for explanation, but if that thoroughbred knew where the major had permanently put the last batch of his furniture, he, too, gave no outward sign.

As for the servants, were there not old Rachel and Sam, chef and valet? What more could one want? The major's voice, too, had lost none of its persuasive powers.

"Here, Sam, you black imp, carry yo' Marster Jack's gun and things to my room, and, Rachel, take the colonel's bag to the sea-room, next to the dinin'-hall. Breakfast in an hour, gentlemen, as Mrs. Slocomb used to say."

I found only a bed covered with a quilt, an old table with small drawers, a wash-stand, two chairs, and a desk on three legs. The walls were bare except for a fly-stained map yellow with age. As I passed through the sitting-room, Rachel preceding me with my traps, I caught a glimpse of traces of better times. There was a plain wooden mantelpiece, a wide fireplace with big brass andirons, a sideboard with and without brass handles and a limited number of claw feet, — which if brought under the spell of the scraper and varnish-pot might once more regain its lost estate, — a corner-cupboard built into the wall, half full of fragments of old china, and, to do justice to the major's former statement, there was also a pair of dull old mahogany doors with glass knobs separating the room from some undiscovered unknown territory of bareness and emptiness beyond. These, no doubt, were the doors Anthony threw open for the bevies of beauties so picturesquely described by the major, but where were the Chippendale furniture, the George III. silver, the Italian marble mantels with carved lions' heads, the marquetry floors and cabinets?

I determined to end my mental suspense. I would ask Rachel and get at the facts. The old woman was opening the windows, letting in the fresh breath of a honeysuckle, and framing a view of the sea beyond.

"How long have you lived here, aunty?"

"'Most fo'ty years, sah. Long 'fo' Massa John Talbot died."

"Where's old Anthony?" I said.

"What Anthony? De fust major's body-servant?"

"Yes."

"Go 'long, honey. He's daid dese twenty years. Daid two years 'fo' Massa Slocomb married Mis' Talbot."

"And Anthony never waited at all on Major Slocomb?"

"How could he wait on him, honey, when he daid 'fo' he see him?"

I pondered for a moment over the picturesque quality of the major's mendacity.

Was it, then, only another of the major's tributes to his wife,—this whole story of Anthony and the madeira of '39? How he must have loved this dear relic of his military predecessor!

An hour later the major strolled into the sitting-room, his arm through Jack's.

"Grand old place, is it not?" he said, turning to me. "Full of historic interest. Of co'se the damnable oligarchy has stripped us, but"—

Here Aunt Rachel flopped in—her slippers, I mean; the sound was distinctly audible.

"Bre'kfus', major."

"All right, Rachel. Come, gentlemen!"

When we were all seated, the major leaned back in his chair, toyed with his knife a moment, and said with an air of great deliberation:—

"Gentlemen, when I was in New York I discovered that the fashionable dish of the day was a po'ter-house steak. So when I knew you were coming, I wired my agent in Baltimo' to go to Lexington market and to send me down on ice the best steak he could buy fo' money. It is now befo' you.

"Jack, shall I cut you a piece of the tenderloin?"

A KNIGHT OF THE LEGION OF HONOR

It was in the smoking-room of a Cunarder two days out. The evening had been spent in telling stories, the fresh-air passengers crowding the doorways to listen, the habitual loungers and card-players abandoning their books and games.

When my turn came,—mine was a story of Venice, a story of the old palace of the Barbarozzi,—I noticed in one corner of the room a man seated alone wrapped in a light shawl, who had listened intently as he smoked, but who took no part in the general talk. He attracted my attention from his likeness to my friend Vereschagin the painter; his broad, white forehead, finely wrought features, clear, honest, penetrating eye, flowing mustache and beard streaked with gray,—all strongly suggestive of that distinguished Russian. I love Vereschagin, and so, unconsciously, and by mental association, perhaps, I was drawn to this stranger. Seeing my eye fixed constantly upon him, he threw off his shawl, and crossed the room.

"Pardon me, but your story about the Barbarozzi brought to my mind so many delightful recollections that I cannot help thanking you. I know that old palace,—knew it thirty years ago,—and I know that cortile, and although I have not had the good fortune to run across either your gondolier, Espero, or his sweetheart, Mariana, I have known a dozen others as romantic and delightful. The air is stifling here. Shall we have our coffee outside on the deck?"

When we were seated, he continued, "And so you are going to Venice to paint?"

"Yes; and you?"

"Me? Oh, to the Engadine to rest. American life is so exhausting that I must have these three months of quiet to make the other nine possible."

The talk drifted into the many curious adventures befalling a man in his journeyings up and down the world, most of them suggested by the queer stories of the night. When coffee had been served, he lighted another cigar, held the match until it burned itself out,—the yellow flame lighting up his handsome face,—looked out over the broad expanse of tranquil sea, with its great highway of silver leading up to the full moon dominating the night, and said as if in deep thought:—

"And so you are going to Venice?" Then, after a long pause: "Will you mind if I tell you of an adventure of my own,—one still most vivid in my memory? It happened near there many years ago." He picked up his shawl, pushed our chairs close to the overhanging life-boat, and continued: "I had begun my professional career, and had gone abroad to study the hospital system in Europe. The revolution in Poland—the revolt of '62—had made traveling in northern Europe uncomfortable, if not dangerous, for foreigners, even with the most authentic of passports, and so I had spent the summer in Italy. One morning, early in the autumn, I bade good-by to my gondolier at the water-steps of the railroad station, and bought a ticket for Vienna. An important letter required my immediate presence in Berlin.

"On entering the train I found the carriage occupied by two persons: a lady, richly dressed, but in deep mourning and heavily veiled; and a man, dark and smooth-faced, wearing a high silk hat. Raising my cap, I placed my umbrella and smaller traps under the seat, and hung my bundle of traveling shawls in the rack overhead. The lady returned my salutation gravely, lifting her veil and making room for my bundles. The dark man's only response was a formal touching of his hat-brim with his forefinger.

"The lady interested me instantly. She was perhaps twenty-five years of age, graceful, and of distinguished bearing. Her hair was jet-black, brushed straight back from her temples, her complexion a rich olive, her teeth pure white. Her lashes were long, and opened and shut with a slow, fan-like movement, shading a pair of deep blue eyes, which shone with that peculiar light only seen when quick tears lie hidden under half-closed lids. Her figure was rounded and full, and her hands exquisitely modeled. Her dress, while of the richest material, was perfectly plain, with a broad white collar and cuffs like those of a nun. She wore no jewels of any kind. I judged her to be a woman of some distinction,—an Italian or Hungarian, perhaps.

"When the train started, the dark man, who had remained standing, touched his hat to me, raised it to the lady, and disappeared. Her only acknowledgment was a slight inclination of the head. A polite stranger, no doubt, I thought, who prefers the smoker. When the train stopped for luncheon, I noticed that the lady did not leave the carriage, and on my return I found her still seated, looking listlessly out of the window, her head upon her hand.

"'Pardon me, madame,' I said in French, 'but unless you travel some distance this is the last station where you can get anything to eat.'

"She started, and looked about helplessly. 'I am not hungry. I cannot eat—but I suppose I should.'

"'Permit me;' and I sprang from the carriage, and caught a waiter with a tray before the guard reclosed the doors. She drank the coffee, tasted the fruit, thanking me in a low, sweet voice, and said:—

"'You are very considerate. It will help me to bear my journey. I am very tired, and weaker than I thought; for I have not slept for many nights.'

"I expressed my sympathy, and ended by telling her I hoped we could keep the carriage to ourselves; she might then sleep undisturbed. She looked at me fixedly, a curious startled expression crossing her face, but made no reply.

"Almost every man is drawn, I think, to a sad or tired woman. There is a look about the eyes that makes an instantaneous draft on the sympathies. So, when these slight confidences of my companion confirmed my misgivings as to her own weariness, I at once began diverting her as best I could with some account of my summer's experience in Venice, and with such of my plans for the future as at the moment filled my mind. I was younger then,—perhaps only a year or two her senior,—and you know one is not given to much secrecy at twenty-six: certainly not with a gentle lady whose goodwill you are trying to gain, and whose sorrowful face, as I have said, enlists your sympathy at sight. Then, to establish some sort of footing for myself, I drifted into an account of my own home life; telling her of my mother and sisters, of the social customs of our country, of the freedom given the women,—so different from what I had seen abroad,—of their perfect safety everywhere.

"We had been talking in this vein some time, she listening quietly until something I said reacted in a slight curl of her lips,—more incredulous than contemptuous, perhaps, but significant all the same; for, lifting her eyes, she answered slowly and meaningly:—

"'It must be a paradise for women. I am glad to believe that there is one corner of the earth where they are treated with respect. My own experiences have been so different that I have begun to believe that none of us are safe after we leave our cradles.' Then, as if suddenly realizing the inference, the color mounting to her cheeks, she added: 'But please do not misunderstand me. I am quite willing to accept your statement; for I never met an American before.'

"As we neared the foothills the air grew colder. She instinctively drew her cloak the closer, settling herself in one corner and closing her eyes wearily. I offered my rug, insisting that she was not properly clad for a journey over the mountains at night. She refused gently but firmly, and closed her eyes again, resting her head against the dividing cushion. For a moment I watched her; then arose from my seat, and, pulling down my bundle of shawls, begged that I might spread my heaviest rug over her lap. An angry color mounted to her cheeks. She turned upon me, and was about to refuse indignantly, when I interrupted: —

"'Please allow me; don't you know you cannot sleep if you are cold? Let me put this wrap about you. I have two.'

"With the unrolling, the leather tablet of the shawl-strap, bearing my name, fell in her lap.

"'Your name is Bosk,' she said, with a quick start, 'and you an American?'

"'Yes; why not?'

"'My maiden name is Boski,' she replied, looking at me in astonishment, 'and I am a Pole.'

"Here were two mysteries solved. She was married, and neither Italian nor Slav.

"'And your ancestry?' she continued with increased animation. 'Are you of Polish blood? You know our name is a great name in Poland. Your grandfather, of course, was a Pole.' Then, with deep interest, 'What are your armorial bearings?'

"I answered that I had never heard that my grandfather was a Pole. It was quite possible, though, that we might be of Polish descent, for my father had once told me of an ancestor, an old colonel, who fell at Austerlitz. As to the armorial bearings, we Americans never cared for such things. The only thing I could remember was a certain seal which my father used to wear, and with which he sealed his letters. The tradition in the family was that it belonged to this old colonel. My sister used it sometimes. I had a letter from her in my pocket.

"She examined the indented wax on the envelope, opened her cloak quickly, and took from the bag at her side a seal mounted in jewels, bearing a crest and coat of arms.

"'See how slight the difference. The quarterings are almost the same, and the crest and motto identical. This side is mine, the other is my husband's. How very, very strange! And yet you are an American?'

"'And your husband's crest?' I asked. 'Is he also a Pole?'

"'Yes; I married a Pole,' with a slight trace of haughtiness, even resentment, at the inquiry.

"'And his name, madame? Chance has given you mine — a fair exchange is never a robbery.'

"She drew herself up, and said quickly, and with a certain bearing I had not noticed before: —

"'Not now; it makes no difference.'

"Then, as if uncertain of the effect of her refusal, and with a willingness to be gracious, she added: —

"In a few minutes — at ten o'clock — we reach Trieste. The train stops twenty minutes. You were so kind about my luncheon; I am stronger now. Will you dine with me?'

"I thanked her, and on arriving at Trieste followed her to the door. As we alighted from the carriage I noticed the same dark man standing by the steps, his fingers on his hat. During the meal my companion seemed brighter and less weary, more gracious and friendly, until I called the waiter and counted out the florins on his tray. Then she laid her hand quietly but firmly upon my arm.

"'Please do not — you distress me; my servant Polaff has paid for everything.'

"I looked up. The dark man was standing behind her chair, his hat in his hand.

"I can hardly express to you my feelings as these several discoveries revealed to me little by little the conditions and character of my traveling companion. Brought up myself under a narrow home influence, with only a limited knowledge of the world, I had never yet been thrown in with a woman of her class. And yet I cannot say that it was altogether the charm of her person that moved me. It was more a certain hopeless sort of sorrow that seemed to envelop her, coupled with an indefinable distrust which I could not solve. Her reserve, however, was impenetrable, and her guarded silence on every subject bearing upon herself so pronounced that I dared not break through it. Yet, as she sat there in the carriage after dinner, during the earlier hours of the night, she and I the only occupants, her eyes heavy and red for want of sleep, her beautiful hair bound in a veil, the pallor of her skin intensified by the sombre hues of her dress, I would have given anything in the world to have known her well enough to have comforted her, even by a word.

"As the night wore on the situation became intolerable. Every now and then she would start from her seat, jostled awake by the roughness of the road,—this section had just been completed,—turn her face the other way, only to be awakened again.

"'You cannot sleep. May I make a pillow for your head of my other shawl? I do not need it. My coat is warm enough.'

"'No; I am very comfortable.'

"'Forgive me, you are not. You are very uncomfortable, and it pains me to see you so weary. These dividing-irons make it impossible for you to lie down. Perhaps I can make a cushion for your head so that you will rest easier.'

"She looked at me coldly, her eyes riveted on mine.

"'You are very kind, but why do you care? You have never seen me before, and may never again.'

"'I care because you are a woman, alone and unprotected. I care most because you are suffering. Will you let me help you?'

"She bent her head, and seemed wrapped in thought. Then straightening up, as if her mind had suddenly resolved,—

"'No; leave me alone. I will sleep soon. Men never really care for a woman when she suffers.' She turned her face to the window.

"'I pity you, then, from the bottom of my heart,' I replied, nettled at her remark. 'There is not a man the length and breadth of my land who would not feel for you now as I do, and there is not a woman who would misunderstand him.'

"She raised her head, and in a softened voice, like a sorrowing child's, it was so pathetic, said: 'Please forgive me. I had no right to speak so. I shall be very grateful to you if you can help me; I am so tired.'

"I folded the shawl, arranged the rug over her knees, and took the seat beside her. She thanked me, laid her cheek upon the impromptu pillow, and closed her eyes. The train sped on, the carriage swaying as we rounded the curves, the jolting increasing as we neared the great tunnel. Settling myself in my seat, I drew my traveling-cap well down so that its shadow from the overhead light would conceal my eyes, and watched her unobserved. For half an hour I followed every line in her face, with its delicate nostrils, finely cut nose, white temples with their blue veins, and the beautiful hair glistening in the half-shaded light, the long lashes resting, tired out, upon her cheek. Soon I noticed at irregular intervals a nervous twitching pass over her face; the brow would knit and relax wearily, the mouth droop. These indications of extreme exhaustion occurred constantly, and alarmed me. Unchecked, they would result in an alarming form of nervous prostration. A sudden lurch dislodged the pillow.

"'Have you slept?' I asked.

"'I do not know. A little, I think. The car shakes so.'

"'My dear lady,' I said, laying my hand on hers, — she started, but did not move her own, — 'it is absolutely necessary that you sleep, and at once. What your nervous strain has been, I know not; but my training tells me that it has been excessive, and still is. Its continuance is dangerous. This road gets rougher as the night passes. If you will rest your head upon my shoulder, I can hold you so that you will go to sleep.'

"Her face flushed, and she recovered her hand quickly.

"'You forget, sir, that' —

"'No, no; I forget nothing. I remember everything; that I am a stranger, that you are ill, that you are rapidly growing worse, that, knowing as I do your condition, I cannot sit here and not help you. It would be brutal.'

"Her lips quivered, and her eyes filled. 'I believe you,' she said. Then, turning quickly with an anxious look, 'But it will tire you.'

"'No; I have held my mother that way for hours at a time.'

"She put out her hand, laid it gently on my wrist, looked into my face long and steadily, scanning every feature, as if reassuring herself, then laid her cheek upon my shoulder, and fell asleep.

"When the rising sun burst behind a mountain-crag, and, at a turn in the road, fell full upon her face, she awoke with a start, and looked about bewildered. Then her mind cleared.

"'How good you have been. You have not moved all night so I might rest. I awoke once frightened, but your hands were folded in your lap.'

"With this her whole manner changed. All the haughty reserve was gone; all the cynicism, the distrust, and suspicion. She became as gentle and tender as an anxious mother, begging me to go to sleep at once. She would see that no one disturbed me. It was cruel that I was so exhausted.

"When the guard entered, she sent for her servant, and bade him watch out for a pot of coffee at the next station. 'To think monsieur had not slept all night!' When Polaff handed in the tray, she filled the cups herself, adding the sugar, and insisting that I should also drink part of her own,—one cup was not enough. Upon Polaff's return she sent for her dressing-case. She must make her toilet at once, and not disturb me. It would be several hours before we reached Vienna; she felt sure I would sleep now.

"I watched her as she spread a dainty towel over the seat in front, and began her preparations, laying out the powder-boxes, brushes, and comb, the bottles of perfume, and the little knickknacks that make up the fittings of a gentlewoman's boudoir. It was almost with a show of enthusiasm that she picked up one of the bottles, and pointed out to me again the crest in relief upon its silver top, saying over and over again how glad she was to know that some of her own blood ran in my veins. She was sure now that I belonged to her mother's people. When, at the next station, Polaff brought a basin of water, and I arose to leave the car, she begged me to remain, — the toilet was nothing; it would be over in a minute. Then she loosened her hair, letting it fall in rich masses about her shoulders, and bathed her face and hands, rearranging her veil, and adding a fresh bit of lace to her throat. I remember distinctly how profound an impression this strange scene made upon my mind, so different from any former experience of my life, — its freedom from conventionality, the lack of all false modesty, the absolute absence of any touch of coquetry or conscious allurement.

"When it was all over, her beauty being all the more pronounced now that the tired, nervous look had gone out of her face, she still talked on, saying how much better and fresher she felt, and how much more rested than the night before. Suddenly her face saddened, and for many minutes she kept silence, gazing dreamily down into the abysses white with the rush of Alpine torrents, or hidden in the early morning fog. Then, finding I would not sleep, and with an expression as if she had finally resolved upon some definite action, and with a face in which every line showed the sincerest confidence and trust, — as unexpected as it was incomprehensible to me, — she said: —

"'Last night you asked me for my name. I would not tell you then. Now you shall know. I am the Countess de Rescka Smolenski. I live in Cracow. My husband died in Venice four days ago. I took him there because he was ill, — so ill that he was carried in Polaff's arms from the gondola to his bed. The Russian government permitted me to take him to Italy to die. One Pole the less is of very little consequence. A week ago this permit was revoked, and we were ordered to report at Cracow without delay. Why, I do not know, except perhaps to add another cruelty to the long list of wrongs the government have heaped upon my family. My husband lingered three days with the order spread out on the table beside him. The fourth day they laid him in Campo Santo. That night my maid fell ill. Yesterday morning a second peremptory order was handed me. I am now on my way home to obey.'

"Then followed in slow, measured sentences the story of her life: married at seventeen at her father's bidding to a man twice her age;

surrounded by a court the most dissolute in eastern Europe; forced into a social environment that valued woman only as a chattel, and that ostracized or defamed every wife who, reverencing her womanhood, protested against its excesses. For five years past—ever since her marriage—her husband's career had been one long, unending dissipation. At last, broken down by a life he had not the moral courage to resist, he had succumbed and taken to his bed; thence, wavering between life and death, like a burnt-out candle flickering in its socket, he had been carried to Venice.

"'Do you wonder, now, that my faith is gone, my heart broken?'

"We were nearing Vienna; the stations were more frequent; our own carriage began filling up. For an hour we rode side by side, silent, she gazing fixedly from the window, I half stunned by this glimpse of a life the pathos of which wrung my very heart. When we entered the station she roused herself, and said to me half pleadingly:—

"'I cannot bear to think I may never see you again. To-night I must stay in Vienna. Will you dine with me at my hotel? I go to the Metropole. And you? Where did you intend to go?'

"'To the Metropole, also.'

"'Not when you left Venice?'

"'Yes; before I met you.'

"'There is a fate that controls us,' she said reverently. 'Come at seven.'

"When the hour arrived I sent my card to her apartment, and was ushered into a small room with a curtain-closed door opening out into a larger salon, through which I caught glimpses of a table spread with glass and silver. Polaff, rigid and perpendicular, received me with a stiff, formal recognition. I do not think he quite understood, nor altogether liked, his mistress's chance acquaintance. In a moment she entered from a door opposite, still in her black garments with the nun's cuffs and broad collar. Extending her hand graciously, she said:—

"'You have slept since I left you this morning. I see it in your face. I am so glad. And I too. I have rested all day. It was so good of you to come.'

"There was no change in her manner; the same frank, trustful look in her eyes, the same anxious concern about me. When dinner was announced she placed me beside her, Polaff standing behind her chair, and the other attendants serving.

"The talk drifted again into my own life, she interrupting with pointed questions, and making me repeat again and again the stories I told her of our humble home. She must learn them herself to tell them to her own people, she said. It was all so strange and new to her, so simple and so genuine. With the coffee she fell to talking of her own home, the despotism of Russia, the death of her father, the forcing of her brothers into the army. Still holding her cup in her hands, she began pacing up and down, her eyes on the floor (we were alone, Polaff having retired). Then stopping in front of me, and with an earnestness that startled me: —

"'Do not go to Berlin. Please come to Cracow with me. Think. I am alone, absolutely alone. My house is in order, and has been for months, expecting me every day. It is so terrible to go back; come with me, please.'

"'I must not, madame. I have promised my friends to be in Berlin in two days. I would, you know, sacrifice anything of my own to serve you.'

"'And you will not?' and a sigh of disappointment escaped her.

"'I cannot.'

"'No; I must not ask you. You are right. It is better that you keep your word.'

"She continued walking, gazing still on the floor. Then she moved to the mantel, and touched a bell. Instantly the curtains of the door divided, and Polaff stood before her.

"'Bring me my jewel-case.'

"The man bowed gravely, looked at me furtively from the corner of his eye, and closed the curtains behind him. In a moment he returned, bearing a large, morocco-covered box, which he placed on the table. She pressed the spring, and the lid flew up, uncovering several velvet-lined trays filled with jewels that flashed under the lighted candles.

"'You need not wait, Polaff. You can go to bed.'

"The man stepped back a pace, stood by the wall, fixed his eye upon his mistress, as if about to speak, looked at me curiously, then, bowing low, drew the curtains aside, and closed the door behind him.

"Another spring, and out came a great string of pearls, a necklace of sapphires, some rubies, and emeralds. These she heaped up upon the white cloth beside her. Carefully examining the contents of the case, she drew from a lower tray a bracelet set with costly diamonds, a rare and beautiful ornament, and before I was aware of her intent had clasped it upon my wrist.

"'I want you to wear this for me. You see it is large enough to go quite up the arm."

"For a moment my astonishment was so great I could not speak. Then I loosened it and laid it in her hand again. She looked up, her eyes filling, her face expressive of the deepest pain.

"'And you will not?'

"'I cannot, madame. In my country men do not accept such costly presents from women, and then we do not wear bracelets, as your men do here.'

"'Then take this case, and choose for yourself.'

"I poured the contents of a small tray into my hand, and picked out a plain locket, almond-shaped, simply wrought, with an opening on one side for hair.

"'Give me this with your hair.'

"She threw the bracelet into the case, and her eyes lighted up.

"'Oh, I am so glad, so glad! It was mine when I was a child, — my mother gave it to me. The dear little locket — yes; you shall always wear it.'

"Then, rising from her seat, she took my hands in hers, and, looking down into my face, said, her voice breaking: —

"'It is eleven o'clock. Soon you must leave me. You cannot stay longer. I know that in a few hours I shall never see you again. Will you join me in my prayers before I go?'

"A few minutes later she called to me. She was on her knees in the next room, two candles burning beside her, her rich dark hair loose about her shoulders, an open breviary bound with silver in her hands. I can see her now, with her eyes closed, her lips moving noiselessly, her great lashes wet with tears, and that Madonna-like look as she motioned me to kneel. For several minutes she prayed thus, the candles lighting her face, the room deathly still. Then she arose, and with her eyes half shut, and her lips moving as if with her unfinished prayer, she lifted her head and kissed me on the forehead, on the chin, and on each cheek, making with her finger the sign of the cross. Then, reaching for a pair of scissors, and cutting a small tress from her hair, she closed the locket upon it, and laid it in my hand.

"Early the next morning I was at her door. She was dressed and waiting. She greeted me kindly, but mournfully, saying in a tone which denoted her belief in its impossibility: —

"'And you will not go to Cracow?'

"When we reached the station, and I halted at the small gate opening upon the train platform, she merely pressed my hand, covered her head with her veil, and entered the carriage followed by Polaff. I watched, hoping to see her face at the window, but she remained hidden.

"I turned into the Ringstrasse, still filled with her presence, and tortured by the thought of the conditions that prevented my following her, called a cab, and drove to our minister's. Mr. Motley then held the portfolio; my passport had expired, and, as I was entering Germany, needed renewing. The attaché agreed to the necessity, stamped it, and brought it back to me with the ink still wet.

"'His excellency,' said he, 'advises extreme caution on your part while here. Be careful of your associates, and keep out of suspicious company. Vienna is full of spies watching escaped Polish refugees.

Your name'—reading it carefully—'is apt to excite remark. We are powerless to help in these cases. Only last week an American who befriended a man in the street was arrested on the charge of giving aid and comfort to the enemy, and, despite our efforts, is still in prison.'

"I thanked him, and regained my cab with my head whirling. What, after all, if the countess should have deceived me? My blood chilled as I remembered her words of the day before: recalled by the government she hated, her two brothers forced into the army, the cruelties and indignities Russia had heaped upon her family, and this last peremptory order to return. Had my sympathetic nature and inexperience gotten me into trouble? Then that Madonna-like head with angelic face, the lips moving in prayer, rose before me. No, no; not she. I would stake my life.

"I entered my hotel, and walked across the corridor for the key of my room. Standing by the porter was an Austrian officer in full uniform, even to his white kid gloves. As I passed I heard the porter say in German:—

"'Yes; that is the man.'

"The Austrian looked at me searchingly, and, wheeling around sharply, said:—

"'Monsieur, can I see you alone? I have something of importance to communicate.'

"The remark and his abrupt manner indicated so plainly an arrest, that for the moment I hesitated, running over in my mind what might be my wisest course to pursue. Then, thinking I could best explain my business in Vienna in the privacy of my room, *I* said stiffly:—

"'Yes; I am now on my way to my apartment. I will see you there.'

"He entered first, shut the door behind him, crossed the room; passed his hand behind the curtains, opened the closet, shut it, and said:—

"'We are alone?'

"'Quite.'

"Then, confronting me, 'You are an American?'

"'You are right.'

"'And have your passport with you?'

"I drew it from my pocket, and handed it to him. He glanced at the signature, refolded it, and said: —

"'You took the Countess Smolensk! to the station this morning. Where did you meet her?'

"'On the train yesterday leaving Venice.'

"'Never before?'

"'Never.'

"'Why did she not leave Venice earlier?'

"'The count was dying, and could not be moved. He was buried two days ago.'

"A shade passed over his face, 'Poor De Rescka! I suspected as much.'

"Then facing me again, his face losing its suspicious expression: —

"'Monsieur, I am the brother of the countess, — Colonel Boski of the army. A week ago my letters were intercepted, and I left Cracow in the night. Since then I have been hunted like an animal. This uniform is my third disguise. As soon as my connection with the plot was discovered, my sister was ordered home. The death of the count explains her delay, and prevented my seeing her at the station. I had selected the first station out of Vienna. I tried for an opportunity this morning at the depot, but dared not. I saw you, and learned from the cabman your hotel.'

"'But, colonel,' said I, the attaché's warning in my ears, 'you will pardon me, but these are troublous times. I am alone here, on my way to Berlin to pursue my studies. I found the countess ill and suffering, and unable to sleep. She interested me profoundly, and I did what I could to relieve her. I would have done the same for any other woman in her condition the world over, no matter what the consequences. If you are her brother, you will appreciate this. If you are here for any other purpose, say so at once. I leave Vienna at noon.'

"His color flushed, and his hand instinctively felt for his sword; then, relaxing, he said:—

"'You are right. The times are troublous. Every other man is a spy. I do not blame you for suspecting me. I have nothing but my word. If you do not believe it, I cannot help it. I will go. You will at least permit me to thank you for your kindness to my sister,' drawing off his glove and holding out his hand.

"'The hand of a soldier is never refused the world over,' and I shook it warmly. As it dropped to his side I caught sight of his seal-ring.

"'Pardon me one moment. Give me your hand again.' The ring bore the crest and motto of the countess.

"'It is enough, colonel. Your sister showed me her own on the train. Pardon my suspicions. What can I do for you?' He looked puzzled, hardly grasping my meaning.

"'Nothing. You have told me all I wanted to know.'

"'But you will breakfast with me before I take the train?' I said.

"'No; that might get you into trouble—serious trouble, if I should be arrested. On the contrary, I must insist that you remain in this room until I leave the building.'

"'But you perhaps need money; these disguises are expensive,' glancing at his perfect appointment.

"'You are right. Perhaps twenty rubles—it will be enough. Give me your address in Berlin. If I am taken, you will lose your money. If I escape, it will be returned.'

"I shook his hand, and the door closed. A week later a man wrapped in a cloak called at my lodgings and handed me an envelope. There was no address and no message, only twenty rubles."

I looked out over the sea wrinkling below me like a great sheet of gray satin. The huge life-boat swung above our heads, standing out in strong relief against the sky. After a long pause,—the story had strangely thrilled me,—I asked:—

"Pardon me, have you ever seen or heard of the countess since?"

"Never."

"Nor her brother?"

"Nor her brother."

"And the locket?"

"It is here where she placed it."

At this instant the moon rolled out from behind a cloud, and shone full on his face. He drew out his watch-chain, touched it with his thumb-nail, and placed the trinket in my hand. It was such as a child might wear, an enameled thread encircling it. Through the glass I could see the tiny nest of jet-black hair.

For some moments neither of us spoke. At last, with my heart aglow, my whole nature profoundly stirred by the unconscious nobility of the man, I said: —

"My friend, do you know why she bound the bracelet to your wrist?"

"No; that always puzzled me. I have often wondered."

"She bound the bracelet to your wrist, as of old a maid would have wound her scarf about the shield of her victorious knight, as the queen would pin the iron cross to the breast of a hero. You were the first gentleman she had ever known in her life."

JOHN SANDERS, LABORER

[*The outlines of this story were given me by my friend Augustus Thomas, whose plays are but an index to the tenderness of his own nature.*]

He came from up the railroad near the State line. Sanders was the name on the pay-roll, — John Sanders, laborer. There was nothing remarkable about him. He was like a hundred others up and down the track. If you paid him off on Saturday night you would have forgotten him the next week, unless, perhaps, he had spoken to you. He looked fifty years of age, and yet he might have been but thirty. He was stout and strong, his hair and beard cropped short. He wore a rough blue jumper, corduroy trousers, and a red flannel shirt, which showed at his throat and wrists. He wore, too, a leather strap buckled about his waist.

If there was anything that distinguished him it was his mouth and eyes, especially when he smiled. The mouth was clean and fresh, the teeth snow-white and regular, as if only pure things came through them; the eyes were frank and true, and looked straight at you without wavering. If you gave him an order he said, "Yes, sir," never taking his gaze from yours until every detail was complete. When he asked a question it was to the point and short.

The first week he shoveled coal on a siding, loading the yard engines. Then Burchard, the station-master, sent him down to the street crossing to flag the trains for the dump carts filling the scows at the long dock.

This crossing right-angled a deep railroad cut half a mile long. On the level above, looking down upon its sloping sides, staggered a row of half-drunken shanties with blear-eyed windows, and ragged roofs patched and broken; some hung over on crutches caught under their floor timbers. Sanders lived in one of these cabins,—the one nearest the edge of the granite retaining-wall flanking the street crossing.

Up the slopes of this railroad cut lay the refuse of the shanties,— bottomless buckets, bits of broken chairs, tomato cans, rusty hoops, fragments of straw matting, and other debris of the open lots. In the summer-time a few brave tufts of grass, coaxed into life by the warm sun, clung desperately to an accidental level, and now and then a gay dandelion flamed for a day or two and then disappeared, cut off by some bedouin goat. In the winter there were only patches of blackened snow, fouled by the endless smoke of passing trains, and seamed with the short-cut footpaths of the yard men.

There were only two in Sanders's shanty,—Sanders and his crippled daughter, a girl of twelve, with a broken back. She barely reached the sill when she stood at the low window to watch her father waving his flag. Bent, hollow-eyed, shrunken; her red hair cropped short in her neck; her poor little white fingers clutching the window-frame. "The express is late this morning," or "No. 14 is on time," she would say, her restless, eager blue eyes glancing at the clock, or "What a lot of ashes they do be haulin' to-day!" Nothing else was to be seen from her window.

When the whistle blew she took down the dinner-pail, filled it with potatoes and the piece of pork hot from the boiling pot, poured the coffee in the tin cup, put on the cover, and, limping to the edge of the retaining-wall, lowered it over by a string to her father. Sanders looked up and waved his hand, and the girl went back to her post at the window.

When the night came he would light the kerosene lamp in their one room and read aloud the stories from the Sunday papers, she listening eagerly and asking him questions he could not answer, her eyes filling with tears or her face breaking into smiles. This summed up her life.

Not much in the world, all this, for Sanders!—not much of rest, or comfort, or happy sunshine,—not much of song or laughter, the pipe of birds or smell of sweet blossoms,—not much room for gratitude or courage or human kindness or charity. Only the ceaseless engine-bell, the grime, the sulphurous hellish smoke, the driving rain, the ice and dust,—only the endless monotony of ill-smelling, steaming carts, the smoke-stained signal-flag and greasy lantern,—only the tottering shanty with the two beds, the stove, and the few chairs and table,—only the blue-eyed crippled girl who wound her thin arms about his neck.

It was on Sundays in the summer that the dreary monotony ceased. Then Sanders would carry her to the edge of the woods, a mile or more back of the cut. There was a little hollow carpeted with violets, and a pond, where now and then a water-lily escaped the factory boys, and there were big trees and bushes and stretches of grass, ending in open lots squared all over by the sod gatherers.

On these days Sanders would lie on his back and watch the treetops swaying in the sunlight against the sky, and the girl would sit by him and make mounds of fresh mosses and pebbles, and tie the wild flowers into bunches. Sometimes he would pretend that there were fish in the pond, and would cut a pole and bend a pin, tie on a bit of string, and sit for hours watching the cork, she laughing beside him in expectation. Sometimes they would both go to sleep, his arm across her. And so the summer passed.

One day in the autumn, at twelve-o'clock whistle, a crowd of young ruffians from the bolt-works near the brewery swept down the crossing chasing a homeless dog. Sanders stood in the road with his flag. A passing freight train stopped the mob. The dog dashed between the wheels, doubling, and then bounding up the slope of the cut, sprang through the half-open door of the shanty. When he saw the girl he stopped short, hesitated, looked anxiously into her face, crouched flat, and pulling himself along by his paws, laid his head at her feet. When Sanders came home that night the dog was asleep in her lap. He was about to drive him out until he caught the look in her face, then he stopped, and laid his empty dinner-pail on the shelf.

"I seen him a-comin'," he said; "them rats from the bolt-factory was a-humpin' him, too! Guess if the freight hadn't a-come along they'd a-ketched him."

The dog looked wistfully into Sanders's face, scanning him curiously, timidly putting out his paw and dropping it, as if he had been too bold, and wanted to make some sort of a dumb apology, like a poor relation who has come to spend the day. He had never had any respectable ancestors,—none to speak of. You could see that in the coarse, shaggy hair, like a door mat; the awkward ungainly walk, the legs doubling under him; the drooping tail with bare spots down its length, suggesting past indignities. He was not a large dog—only about as high as a chair seat; he had mottled lips, too, and sharp, sawlike teeth. One ear was gone, perhaps in his puppyhood, when some one had tried to make a terrier of him and had stopped when half done. The other ear, however, was active enough for two. It would curl forward in attention like a deer's, or start up like a rabbit's in alarm, or lie back on his head when the girl stroked him to sleep. He was only a kickable, chasable kind of a dog,—a dog made for sounding tin pans tied to his tail and whooping boys behind.

All but his eyes! These were brown as agates, and as deep and clear. Kindly eyes that looked and thought and trusted. It was these eyes that first made the girl love him; they reminded her, strange to say, of her father's. She saw, too, perhaps unconsciously to herself, down in their depths, something of the same hunger for sympathy that stirred her own heart—the longing for companionship. She wanted something nearer her own age to love, though she never told her father. This was a heartache she kept to herself, perhaps because she hardly understood it.

The dog and the girl became inseparable. At night he slept under her bed, reaching his head up in the gray dawn, and licking her face until she covered him up warm beside her. When the trains passed he would stand up on his hind legs, his paws on the sill, his blunt little nose against the pane, whining at the clanging bells, or barking at the great rings of steam and smoke coughed up by the engines below.

She taught him all manner of tricks. How to walk on his hind feet with a paper cap on his head, a plate in his mouth, begging. How to make believe he was dead, lying still a minute at a time, his odd ear furling nervously and his eyes snapping fun; how to carry a basket to the grocery on the corner, when she would limp out in the morning for a penny's worth of milk or a loaf of bread, he waiting until she crossed the street, and then marching on proudly before her.

With the coming of the dog a new and happier light seemed to have brightened the shanty. Sanders himself began to feel the influence. He would play with him by the hour, holding his mouth tight, pushing back his lips so that his teeth glistened, twirling his ear. There was a third person now for him to consult and talk to. "It'll be turrible cold at the crossin' to-day, won't it, Dog?" or, "Thet's No. 23 puffin' up in the cut: don't yer know her bell? Wonder, Dog, what she's switched fur?" he would say to him. He noticed, too, that the girl's cheeks were not so white and pinched. She seemed taller and not so weary; and when he walked up the cut, tired out with the day's work, she always met him at the door, the dog springing half way down the slope, wagging his tail and bounding ahead to welcome him. And she would sing little snatches of songs that her mother had taught her years ago, before the great flood swept away the cabin and left only her father and herself clinging to a bridge, she with a broken back.

After a while Sanders coaxed him down to the track, teaching him to bring back his empty dinner-pail, the dog spending the hour with him, sitting by his side demurely, or asleep in the sentry-box.

All this time the dog never rose to the dignity of any particular name. The girl spoke of him as "Doggie," and Sanders always as "the Dog." The trainmen called him "Rags," in deference, no doubt, to his torn ear and threadbare tail. They threw coal at him as he passed, until it leaked out that he belonged to "Sanders's girl." Then they became his champions, and this name and pastime seemed out of place. Only once did he earn any distinguishing sobriquet. That was when he had saved the girl's basket, after a sharp fight with a larger and less honest dog. Sanders then spoke of him, with half-concealed pride, as "the Boss," but this only lasted a day or so. Publicly, in the neighborhood, he was known as "Sanders's dog."

One morning the dog came limping up the cut with a broken leg. Some said a horse had kicked him; some that the factory boys had thrown stones at him. He made no outcry, only came sorrowfully in, his mouth dry and dust-covered, dragging his hind leg, that hung loose like a flail; then he laid his head in the girl's lap. She crooned and cried over him all day, binding up the bruised limb, washing his eyes and mouth, putting him in her own bed. There was no one to go for her father, and if there were, he could not leave the crossing. When Sanders came home he felt the leg over carefully, the girl watching eagerly. "No, Kate, child, yees can't do nothin'; it's broke at the jint. Don't cry, young one."

Then he went outside and sat on a bench, looking across the cut and over the roofs of the factories, hazy in the breath of a hundred furnaces, and so across the blue river fringed with waving trees where the blessed sun was sinking to rest. He was not surprised. It was like everything else in his life. When he loved something, it was sure to be this way.

That night, when the girl was asleep, he took the dog up in his arms, and wrapping his coat around him so the corner loafers could not see, rang the bell of the dispensary. The doctor was out, but a nurse looked at the wound. "No, there was nothing to be done; the socket had been crushed. Keep it bandaged, that was all." Then he brought him home and put him under the bed.

In three or four weeks he was about again, dragging the leg when he walked. He could still get around the shanty and over to the grocer's, but he could not climb the hill, even with the pail empty.

He tried one day, but he only climbed half way. Sanders found him in the path when he went home, lying down by the pail.

Sanders worried over the dog. He missed the long talks at the crossing over the dinner, the poor fellow sitting by his side watching every spoonful, his eyes glistening, the old ear furling and unfurling like a toy flag. He missed, too, his scampering after the sparrows and pigeons that often braved the desolation and smoke of this inferno to pick up the droppings from the carts. He missed more than all the companionship, — somebody to sit beside him.

As for the girl — there was now a double bond between her and the dog. He was not only poor and an outcast, but a cripple like herself. Before, she was his friend, now, she was his mother, whispering to him, her cheek to his; holding him up to the window to see the trains rush by, his nose touching the glass, his poor leg dangling.

The train hands missed him too, vowing vengeance, and the fireman of No. 6, Joe Connors, spent half a Sunday trying to find the boy that threw the stone. Bill Adams, who ran the yard engine, went all the way home the next day after the accident for a bottle of horse liniment, and left it at the shanty, and said he'd get the doctor at the next station if Sanders wanted.

One broiling hot August day — a day when the grasshoppers sang among the weeds in the open lot, and the tar dripped down from the roofs, when the teams strained up the hill reeking with sweat, a wet sponge over their eyes, and the drivers walked beside their carts mopping their necks — on one of these steaming August days the dog limped down to the crossing just to rub his nose once against Sanders as he stood waving his flag, or to look wistfully up into his face as he sat in the little pepper-box of a house that sheltered his flags and lantern. He did not often come now. They were making up the local freight — the yard engine backing and shunting the cars into line. Bill Adams was at the throttle and Connors was firing. A few yards below Sanders's sentry-box stood an empty flat car on a siding. It threw a grateful shade over the hard cinder-covered tracks. The dog had crawled beneath its trucks and lay asleep, his stiffened leg over the switch frog. Adams's yard engine puffing by woke him with a start. There was a struggle, a yell of pain, and the dog fell over on his back, his useless leg fast in the frog. Sanders heard the cry of agony, threw down his flag, bounded over the cross-ties, and crawled beneath the trucks. The dog's cries stopped. But the leg was fast. In a moment more he had rushed back to his box, caught up a crowbar, and was forcing the joint. It did not give an inch. There was but one thing left — to throw the switch before the express, due in two minutes, whirled past. In another instant a man in a blue jumper was seen darting up the tracks. He sprang at a lever, bounded back, and threw himself under the flat car. Then the yelp of a dog in pain, drowned by the shriek of an engine dashing into the cut at full speed. Then a dog thrown clear of the track, a crash like a falling house, and a flat car smashed into kindling wood.

When the conductor and passengers of the express walked back, Bill Adams was bending over a man in a blue jumper laid flat on the cinders. He was bleeding from a wound in his head. Lying beside him was a yellow dog licking his stiffened hand. A doctor among the passengers opened his red shirt and pressed his hand on the heart. He said he was breathing, and might live. Then they brought a stretcher from the office, and Connors and Bill Adams carried him up the hill, the dog following, limping.

Here they laid him on a bed beside a sobbing, frightened girl; the dog at her feet.

Adams bent over him, washing his head with a wad of cotton waste.

Just before he died he opened his eyes, rested them on his daughter, half raised his head as if in search of the dog, and then fell back on his bed, that same sweet, clear smile about his mouth.

"John Sanders," said Adams, "how in h — - could a sensible man like you throw his life away for a damned yellow dog?"

"Don't, Billy," he said. "I couldn't help it. He was a cripple."

BÄADER

I was sitting in the shadow of Mme. Poulard's delightful inn at St. Michel when I first saw Bäader. Dinner had been served, and I had helped to pay for my portion by tacking a sketch on the wall behind the chair of the hostess. This high valuation was not intended as a special compliment to me, the wall being already covered with similar souvenirs from the sketch-books of half the painters in Europe.

Bäader, he pronounced it Bayder, had at that moment arrived in answer to a telegram from the governor, who the night before, in a moment of desperation, had telegraphed the proprietor of his hotel in Paris, "Send me a courier at once who knows Normandy and speaks English." The bare-headed man who, hat in hand, was at this moment bowing so obsequiously to the governor, was the person who had arrived in response. He was short and thick-set, and perfectly bald on the top of his head in a small spot, friar-fashion. He glistened with perspiration that collected near the hat-line, and escaped in two streams, drowning locks of black hair covering each temple, stranding them like wet grass on his cheek-bones below. His full face was clean-shaven, smug, and persuasive, and framed two shoe-button eyes that, while sharp and alert, lacked neither humor nor tenderness.

He wore a pair of new green kid gloves, was dressed in a brown cloth coat bound with a braid of several different shades, showing different dates of repair, and surmounted by a velvet collar of the same date as the coat. His trousers were of a nondescript gray, and flapped about a pair of brand-new gaiters, evidently purchased for the occasion, and, from the numerous positions assumed while he talked, evidently one size too small.

His hat—the judicious use of which added such warmth, color, and picturesqueness to his style of delivery, now pressed to his chest, now raised aloft, now debased to the cobbles—had once had some dignity and proportions. Continual maltreatment had long since taken all the gay and frolicsome curl out of its brim, while the crown had so often collapsed that the scars of ill-usage were visible upon it. And yet at a distance this relic of a former fashion, as handled by Bäader,—it was so continually in his grasp and so seldom on his head, that you could never say it was worn,—this hat, brushed, polished, and finally slicked by its owner to a state slightly confusing as to whether it were made of polished iron or silk, was really a very gay and attractive affair.

It was easy to see that the person before me had spared neither skill, time, nor expense to make as favorable an impression on his possible employers as lay in his power.

"At the moment of the arrival of ze dépêche télégraphique," Bäader continued, "I was in ze office of monsieur ze propriétaire. It was at ze conclusion of some arrangement commercial, when mon ami ze propriétaire say to me: 'Bäader, it is ze abandoned season in Paris. Why not arrange for ze gentlemen in Normandy? The number of francs a day will be at least'"—here Bäader scrutinized carefully the governor's face—"'at least to ze amount of ten'—is it not so, messieurs? Of course," noting a slight contraction of the eyebrows, "if ze service was of long time, and to ze most far-away point, some abatement could be posseeble. If, par exemple, it was to St. Malo, St. Servan, Paramé, Cancale spéciale, Dieppe petite, Dinard, and ze others, the sum of nine francs would be quite sufficient."

The governor had never heard Dieppe called "petite" nor Cancale "spéciale," and said so, lifting his eyebrows inquiringly. Bäader did not waver. "But if messieurs pretend a much smaller route and of few days, say to St. Michel, Paramé, and Cancale,"—here the governor's brow relaxed again,—"then it was imposseeble,—if messieurs will pardon,—quite imposseeble for less zan ten francs."

So the price was agreed upon, and the hat, now with a decided metallic sheen, once more swept the cobblestones of the courtyard. The ceremony being over, its owner then drew off the green kid gloves, folded them flat on his knee, guided them into the inside pocket of the brown coat with the assorted bindings as carefully as if they had been his letter of credit, and declared himself at our service.

It was when he had been installed as custodian not only of our hand luggage, but to a certain extent of our bank accounts and persons for some days, that he urged upon the governor the advisability of our at once proceeding to Cancale, or Cancale spéciale, as he insisted on calling it. I immediately added my own voice to his pleadings, arguing that Cancale must certainly be on the sea. That, from my recollection of numerous water-colors and black-and-whites labeled in the catalogue, "Coast near Cancale," and the like, I was sure there must be the customary fish-girls, with shrimp-nets carried gracefully over one shoulder, to say nothing of brawny-chested fishermen with flat, rimless caps, having the usual little round button on top.

The governor, however, was obdurate. He had a way of being obdurate when anything irritated him, and Bäader began to be one of these things. Cancale might be all very well for me, but how about the hotel for him, who had nothing to do, no pictures to paint? He had passed that time in his life when he could sleep under a boat with water pouring down the back of his neck through a tarpaulin full of holes.

"The hotel, messieurs! Imagine! Is it posseeble that monsieur imagine for one moment that Bäader would arrange such annoyances? I remember ze hotel quite easily. It is not like, of course, ze Grand Hôtel of Paris, but it is simple, clean, ze cuisine superb, and ze apartment fine and hospitable. Remembare it is Bäader."

"And the baths?" broke out the governor savagely.

Bäader's face was a study; a pained, deprecating expression passed over it as he uncovered his head, his glazed headpiece glistening in the sun.

"Baths, monsieur—and ze water of ze sea everywhere?"

These assurances of future comfort were not overburdened with details, but they served to satisfy and calm the governor, I pleading, meanwhile, that Bäader had always proved himself a man of resource, quite ready when required with either a meal or an answer.

So we started for Cancale.

On the way our courier grew more and more enthusiastic. We were traveling in a four-seated carriage, Bäader on the box, pointing out to us in English, after furtive conversations with the driver in French, the principal points of interest. With many flourishes he led us to Paramé, one of those Normandy cities which consist of a huge hotel with enormous piazzas, a beach ten miles from the sea, and a small so-called fishing-village as a sort of marine attachment. To give a realistic touch, a lone boat is always being tarred somewhere down at the end of one of its toy streets, two or three donkey-carts and donkeys add an air of picturesqueness, and the usual number of children with red pails and shovels dig in the sand of the road-side. All the fish that are sold come from the next town. It was too early in the season when we reached there for girls in sabots and white caps, the tide from Paris not having set in. The governor hailed it with delight. "Why the devil didn't you tell me about this place before? Here we have been fooling away our time."

"But it is only Paramé, monsieur," with an accent on the "only" and a lifting of the hands. "Cancale spéciale will charm you; ze coast it is so immediately flat, and ze life of ze sea charmante. Nevare at Paramé, always at Cancale." So we drove on. The governor pacified but anxious—only succumbing at my argument that Bäader knew all Normandy thoroughly, and that an old courier like him certainly could be trusted to select a hotel.

You all know the sudden dip from the rich, flat country of Normandy down the steep cliffs to the sea. Cancale is like the rest of it. The town itself stands on the brink of a swoop to the sands; the fishing-village proper, where the sea packs it solid in a great half-moon, with a light burning on one end that on clear nights can be seen as far as Mme. Poulard's cozy dining-room at St. Michel.

One glimpse of this sea-burst tumbled me out of the carriage, sketch-trap in hand. Bäader and the governor kept on. If the latter noticed the discrepancy between Bäader's description of the country and the actual topography, no word fell from him at the moment of departure.

From my aerie, as I worked under my white umbrella below the cliff, I could distinctly make out our traveling-carriage several hundred feet below and a mile away, crawling along a road of white tape with a green selvage of trees, the governor's glazed trunk flashing behind, Bäader's silk hat burning in front. Then the little insect stopped at a white spot backed by dots of green; a small speck broke away, and was swallowed up for a few minutes in the white dot,—doubtless Bäader to parley for rooms,—and then to my astonishment the whole insect turned and began crawling back again, growing larger every minute. All this occurred before I had half finished my outline or opened my color-box. Instantly the truth dawned upon me,—the governor was going back to Paramé. An hour, perhaps, had elapsed when Bäader, with uncovered head and beaded with perspiration, the two locks of hair hanging limp and straight, stood before me.

"What was the matter with the governor, Bäader? No hotel after all?"

"On the contraire, pardonnez-moi, monsieur, a most excellent hotel, simple and quite of ze people, and with many patrons. Even at ze moment of arrival a most distinguished artist, a painter of ze Salon, was with his cognac upon a table at ze entrance."

"No bath, perhaps," I remarked casually, still absorbed in my work, and with my mind at rest, now that Bäader remained with me.

"On the contraire, monsieur, les bains are most excellent — primitive, of course, simple, and quite of ze people. But, monsieur le gouverneur is no more young. When one is no more young," — with a deprecating shrug, — "parbleu, it is imposseeble to enjoy everything. Monsieur le gouverneur, I do assure you, make ze conclusion most regretfully to return to Paramé."

I learned the next morning that he evinced every desire to drown Bäader in the surf for bringing him to such an inn, and was restrained only by the knowledge that I should miss his protection during my one night in Cancale.

"Moreover, it is ze grande fête to-night — ze fête of ze République. Zare are fireworks and illumination and music by ze municipality. It is simple, but quite of ze people. It is for zis reason that I made ze effort special with monsieur le gouverneur to remain with you. Ah! it is you, monsieur, who are so robust, so enthusiastic, so appreciative."

Here Bäader put on his hat, and I closed my sketch-trap.

"But monsieur has not yet dined," he said as we walked, "nor even at his hotel arrived. Ze inn of Mme. Flamand is so very far away, and ze ascent up ze cliffs difficile. If monsieur will be so good, zare is a café near by where it is quite posseeble to dine."

Relieved of the governor's constant watchfulness Bäader became himself. He bustled about the restaurant, called for "Cancale spéciale," a variety of oysters apparently entirely unknown to the landlord, and interviewed the *chef* himself. In a few moments a table was spread in a corner of the porch overlooking a garden gay with hollyhocks, and a dinner was ordered of broiled chicken, French rolls, some radishes, half a dozen apricots, and a fragment of cheese. When it was over, — Bäader had been served in an adjoining apartment, — there remained not the amount mentioned in a former out-of-door feast, but sufficient to pack at least one basket, — in this case a paper box, — the drumsticks being stowed below, dunnaged by two rolls, and battened down with fragments of cheese and three apricots.

"What's this for, Bäader? Have you not had enough to eat?"

Bäader's face wore its blandest smile. "On ze contraire, I have made for myself a most excellent repast; but if monsieur will consider — ze dinner is a prix fixe, and monsieur can eat it all, or it shall remain for ze propriétaire. Zis, if monsieur will for one moment attend, will be stupid extraordinaire. I have made ze investigation, and discover zat ze post départ from Cancale in one hour. How simple zen to affeex ze stamps, — only five sous, — and in ze morning, even before Mme. Bäader is out of ze bed, it is in Paris — a souvenir from Cancale. How charmante ze surprise!"

I discovered afterward that since he had joined us Bäader's own domestic larder had been almost daily enriched with crumbs like these from Dives's table.

The *fête,* despite Bäader's assurances, lacked one necessary feature. There was no music. The band was away with the boats, the triangle probably cooking, the French horn and clarinet hauling seines.

But Bäader, not to be outdone by any *contretemps*, started off to find an old blind fellow who played an accordeon, collecting five francs of me in advance for his pay, under the plea that it was quite horrible that the young people could not dance. "While one is young, monsieur, music is ze life of ze heart."

He brought the old man back, and with a certain care and tenderness set him down on a stone bench, the sightless eyes of the poor peasant turning up to the stars as he swayed the primitive instrument back and forth. The young girls clung to Bäader's arm, and blessed him for his goodness. I forgave him his duplicity, his delight in their happiness was so genuine. Perhaps it was even better than a *fête*.

When, later in the evening, we arrived at Mme. Flamand's, we found her in the doorway, her brown face smiling, her white cap and apron in full relief under the glare of an old-fashioned ship's light, which hung from a rafter of the porch. Bäader inscribed my name in a much-thumbed, ink—stained register, which looked like a neglected ship's log, and then added his own. This, by the by, Bäader never neglected. Neither did he neglect a certain little ceremony always connected with it.

After it was all over and "Moritz Bäader Courrier et Interprète" was duly inscribed,—and in justice it must be confessed it was always clearly written with a flourish at the end that lent it additional dignity,—Bäader would pause for a moment, carefully balance the pen, trying it first on his thumb-nail, and then place two little dots of ink over the first *a*, saying, with a certain wave of his hand, as he did so, "For ze honor of my families, monsieur." This peculiarity gained for him from the governor the sobriquet of "old fly-specks."

The inn of Mme. Flamand, although less pretentious than many others that had sheltered us, was clean and comfortable, the lower deck and companionway were freshly sanded,—the whole house had a decidedly nautical air about it,—and the captain's state-room on the upper deck, a second-floor room, was large and well-lighted, although the ceiling might have been a trifle too low for the governor, and the bed a few inches too short.

I ascended to the upper deck, preceded by the hostess carrying the ship's lantern, now that the last guest had been housed for the night. Bäader followed with a brass candlestick and a tallow dip about the size of a lead pencil. With the swinging open of the bedroom door, I made a mental inventory of all the conveniences: bed, two pillows, plenty of windows, washstand, towels. Then the all-important question recurred to me, Where had they hidden the portable tub?

I opened the door of the locker, looked behind a sea-chest, then out of one window, expecting to see the green-painted luxury hanging by a hook or drying on a convenient roof. In some surprise I said: —

"And the bath, Bäader?"

"Does monsieur expect to bathe at ze night?" inquired Bäader with a lifting of his eyebrows, his face expressing a certain alarm for my safety.

"No, certainly not; but to-morrow, when I get up."

"Ah, to-morrow!" with a sigh of relief. "I do assure you, monsieur, zat it will be complete. At ze moment of ze déflexion of monsieur le gouverneur zare was not ze time. Of course it is imposseeble in Cancale to have ze grand bain of Paris, but then zare is still something, — a bath quite spécial, simple, and of ze people. Remember, monsieur, it is Bäader."

And so, with a cheery "Bon soir" from madame, and a profound bow from Bäader, I fell asleep.

The next morning I was awakened by a rumbling in the lower hold, as if the cargo was being shifted. Then came a noise like the moving of heavy barrels on the upper deck forward of the companionway. The next instant my door was burst open, and in stalked two brawny, big-armed fish-girls, yarn-stockinged to their knees, and with white sabots and caps. They were trundling the lower half of a huge hogshead.

"Pour le bain, monsieur," they both called out, bursting into laughter, as they rolled the mammoth tub behind my bed, grounded it with a revolving whirl, as a juggler would spin a plate, and disappeared, slamming the door behind them, their merriment growing fainter as they dropped down the companionway.

I peered over the head-board, and discovered the larger half of an enormous storage-barrel used for packing fish, with fresh saw-marks indenting its upper rim. Then I shouted for Bäader.

Before anybody answered, there came another onslaught, and in burst the same girls, carrying a great iron beach-kettle filled with water. This, with renewed fits of laughter, they dashed into the tub, and in a flash were off again, their wooden sabots clattering down the steps.

There was no mistaking the indications; Bäader's bath had arrived.

I climbed up, and, dropping in with both feet, avoiding the splinters and the nails, sat on the sawed edge, ready for total immersion. Before I could adjust myself to its conditions there came another rush along the companionway, accompanied by the same clatter of sabots and splashing of water. There was no time to reach the bed, and it was equally evident that I could not vault out and throw myself against the door. So I simply ducked down, held on, and shouted, in French, Normandy patois, English:—

"Don't come in! Don't open the door! Leave the water outside!" and the like. I might as well have ruined my throat on a Cancale lugger driving before a gale. In burst the door, and in swept the Amazons, letting go another kettleful, this time over my upper half, my lower half being squeezed down into the tub.

When the girls had emptied the contents of this last kettle over the edge, and caught sight of my face,—they evidently thought I was still behind the head-board,—both gave one prolonged shriek that literally roused the house. The brawnier of the two,—a magnificent creature, with her corsets outside of her dress,—after holding her sides with laughter until I thought she would suffocate, sank upon the sea-chest, from which her companion rescued her just as Mme. Flamand and Bäader opened the door. All this time my chin was resting on the jagged rim of the tub, and my teeth were chattering.

"Bäader, where in thunder have you been? Drag that chest against that door quick, and come in. Is this what you call a bath?"

"Monsieur, if you will pardon. I arouse myself at ze daylight; I rely upon Mme. Flamand that ze Englishman who is dead had left one behind; I search everywhere. Zen I make inquiry of ze mother of ze two demoiselles who have just gone. She was much insulted; she make ze bad face. She say with much indignation: 'Monsieur, since I was a baby ze water has not touched my body.' At ze supreme moment, when all hope was gone, I discover near ze house of ze same madame this grand arrangement. Immediately I am on fire, and say to myself, 'Bäader, all is not lost. Even if zare was still ze bath of ze Englishman, it would not compare.' In ze quickness of an eye I bring a saw, and ze demoiselles are on zare knees making ze arrangement, one part big, one small. I say to myself, 'Bäader, monsieur is an artist, and of enthusiasm, and will appreciate zis utensile agréable of ze fisherman.' If monsieur will consider, it is, of course, not ze grand bain of Paris, but it is simple, and quite of ze people."

Some two months later, the governor and I happened to be strolling through the flower-market of the Madeleine. He had been selecting plants for the windows of his apartment, and needed a reliable man to arrange them in suitable boxes.

"That fellow Bäader lives down here somewhere; perhaps he might know of some one," he said, consulting his notebook. "Yes; No. 21 Rue Chambord. Let us look him up."

In five minutes we stood before a small, two-story house, with its door and wide basement-window protected by an awning. Beneath this, upon low shelves, was arranged a collection of wicker baskets, containing the several varieties of oysters from Normandy and Brittany coasts greatly beloved by Parisian epicures of Paris. On the top of each lid lay a tin sign bearing the name of the exact locality from which each toothsome bivalve was supposed to be shipped. These signs were all of one size.

The governor is a great lover of oysters, especially his own Chesapeakes, and his eye ran rapidly over the tempting exhibit as he read aloud, perhaps, unconsciously, to himself, the several labels: "Dinard, Paramé, Dieppe petite, Cancale spéciale." Then a new light seemed to break in upon him.

"Dieppe petite, Cancale spéciale,"—here his face was a study,— "why, that's what Bäader always called Cancale. By thunder! I believe that's where that fellow got his names. I don't believe the rascal was ever in Normandy in his life until I took him. Here, landlord!" A small shop-keeper, wearing an apron, ran out smiling, uncovering the baskets as he approached. "Do you happen to know a courier by the name of Bäader?"

"Never as courier, messieurs—always as commissionaire; he sells wood and charcoal to ze hotels. See! zare is his sign."

"Where does he live?"

"Upstairs."

THE LADY OF LUCERNE

I

Above the Schweizerhof Hotel, and at the end of the long walk fronting the lake at Lucerne,—the walk studded with the round, dumpy, Noah's-ark trees,—stands a great building surrounded by flowers and palms, and at night ablaze with hundreds of lamps hung in festoons of blue, yellow, and red. This is the Casino. On each side of the wide entrance is a bill-board, announcing that some world-renowned Tyrolean warbler, famous acrobat, or marvelous juggler will sing or tumble or bewilder, the price of admission remaining the same, despite the enormous sum paid for the appearance of the performer.

Inside this everybody's club is a café, with hurrying waiters and a solid brass band, and opening from its smoke and absinthe laden interior blazes a small theatre, with stage footlights and scenery, where the several world-renowned artists redeem at a very considerable discount the promissory notes of the bill-boards outside.

During the performance the audience smoke and sip. Between the acts most of them swarm out into the adjacent corridors leading to the gaming-rooms,—licensed rooms these, with toy-horses ridden by tin jockeys, and another equally delusive and tempting device of the devil—a game of tipsy marbles, rolling about in search of sunken saucers emblazoned with the arms of the nations of the earth. These whirligigs of amateur crime are constantly surrounded by eager-eyed men and women, who try their luck for the amusement of the moment, or by broken-down, seedy gamblers, hazarding their last coin for a turn of fortune. Now and then, too, some sweet-faced girl, her arm in her father's, wins a louis with a franc, her childish laughter ringing out in the stifling atmosphere.

The Tyrolean warbler had just finished her high-keyed falsetto, bowing backward in her short skirts and stout shoes with silver buckles, and I had just reached the long corridor on my way to the garden, to escape the blare and pound of the band, when a man leaned out of a half-opened door and touched my shoulder.

"Pardon, monsieur. May I speak to you a moment?"

He was a short, thick-set, smooth-shaven, greasy man, dressed plainly in black, with a huge emerald pin in his shirt front. I have never had any particular use for a man with an emerald pin in his shirt front.

"There will be a game of baccarat," he continued in a low voice, his eyes glancing about furtively, "at eleven o'clock precisely. Knock twice at this door."

Old habitués of Lucerne—habitués of years, men who never cross the Alps without at least a day's stroll under the Noah's-ark trees,—will tell you over their coffee that since the opening of the St. Gotthard Tunnel this half-way house of Lucerne—this oasis between Paris and Rome—has sheltered most of the adventurers of Europe; that under these same trees, and on these very benches, nihilists have sat and plotted, refugees and outlaws have talked in whispers, and adventuresses, with jeweled stilettos tucked in their bosoms, have lain in wait for fresher victims.

I had never in my wanderings met any of these mysterious and delightful people. And, strange to say, I had never seen a game of baccarat. This might be my opportunity. I would see the game and perhaps run across some of these curious individuals. I consulted my watch; there was half an hour yet. The man was a runner, of course, for this underground, unlicensed gaming-house, who had picked me out as a possible victim.

When the moment arrived I knocked at the door.

It was opened, not by the greasy Jack-in-the-box with the emerald pin, but by a deferential old man, who looked at me for a moment, holding the door with his foot. Then gently closing it, he preceded me across a hall and up a long staircase. At the top was a passage-way and another door, and behind this a large room paneled in dark wood. On one side of this apartment was a high desk. Here sat the cashier counting money, and arranging little piles of chips of various colors. In the centre stood a table covered with black cloth: I had always supposed such tables to be green. About it were seated ten people, the croupier in the middle. The game had already begun. I moved up a chair, saying that I would look on, but not play.

Had the occasion been a clinic, the game a corpse, and the croupier the operating surgeon, the group about the table could not have been more absorbed or more silent; a cold, death-like, ominous stillness that seemed to saturate the very air. The only sounds were the occasional clickings of the ivory chips, like the chattering of teeth, and the monotones of the croupier announcing the results of the play: —

"Faites vos jeux. Le jeu est fait; rien ne va plus."

I began to study the *personnel* of this clinic of chance.

Two Englishmen in evening dress sat side by side, never speaking, scarcely moving, their eyes riveted on the falling cards flipped from the croupier's hands. A coarse-featured, oily-skinned woman — a Russian, I thought — looked on calmly, resting her head on her palm. A man in a gray suit, with waxy face and watery, yellow eyes, made paper pills, rolling them slowly between thumb and forefinger — his features as immobile as a death-mask. A blue-eyed, blond German officer, with a decoration on the lapel of his coat, nonchalantly twirled his mustache, his shoulders straining in tension. A Parisienne, with bleached hair and penciled eyebrows, leaned over her companion's arm. There was also a flashily dressed negro, evidently a Haytian, who sat motionless at the far end, as stolid as a boiler, only the steam-gauge of his eyes denoting the pressure beneath.

No one spoke, no one laughed.

Two of the group interested me at once, — the croupier and a woman who sat within three feet of me.

The croupier, who was in evening dress, might have been of any age from thirty to fifty. His eyes were deep-set and glassy, like those of a consumptive. His hair was jet-black, his face clean-shaven; the skin, not ivory, but a dirty white, and flabby, like the belly of a toad. His thin and bloodless lips were flattened over a row of pure white teeth with glistening specks of gold that opened when he smiled; closing again slowly like an automaton's. His shrunken, colorless hands lay on the black cloth like huge white spiders; their long, thin legs of fingers turned up at the tips — stealthy, creeping fingers. Sometimes, too, in their nervous workings, they drooped together like a bunch of skeleton keys. On one of these lock picks he wore a ring studded alternately with diamonds and rubies.

The cards seemed to know these fingers, fluttering about them, or lighting noiselessly at their bidding on the cloth.

When the bank won, the croupier permitted a slight shade of disappointment to flash over his face, fading into an expression of apology for taking the stakes. When the bank lost, the lips parted slowly, showing the teeth, in a half smile. Such delicate outward consideration for the feelings of his victims seemed a part of his education, an index to his natural refinement.

The woman was of another type. Although she sat with her back to me, I could catch her profile when she pushed her long veil from her face. She was dressed entirely in black. She had been, and was still, a woman of marked beauty, with an air of high breeding which was unmistakable. Her features were clean-cut and refined, her mouth and nose delicately shaped. Her forehead was shaded by waves of brown hair which half covered her ears. The eyes were large and softened by long lashes, the lids red as if with recent weeping. Her only ornament was a plain gold ring, worn on her left hand. Outwardly, she was the only person in the room who betrayed by her manner any vital interest in the game.

There are some faces that once seen haunt you forever afterward—faces with masks so thinly worn that you look through into the heart below. Hers was one of these. Every light and shadow of hope and disappointment that crossed it showed only the clearer the intensity of her mental strain, and the bitterness of her anxiety.

Once when she lost she bit her lips so deeply that a speck of blood tinged her handkerchief. The next instant she was clutching her winnings with almost the ferocity of a hungry animal. Then she leaned back a moment later exhausted in her chair, her face thrown up, her eyes closing wearily.

In her hand she held a small chamois bag filled with gold; when her chips were exhausted she would rise silently, float like a shadow to the desk, lay a handful of gold from the bag upon the counter, sweep the ivories into her hand, and noiselessly regain her seat. She seemed to know no one, and no one to know her, unless it might have been the croupier, who, I thought, watched her closely when he pushed over her winnings, parting his lips a little wider, his smile a trifle more cringing and devilish.

At twelve o'clock she was still playing, her face like chalk, her eyes bloodshot, her teeth clenched fast, her hair disheveled across her face.

The game went on.

When the clock reached the half-hour the man in gray pushed back his chair, gathered up his winnings, and moved to the door, an attendant handing him his hat. With the exception of the Parisienne, who had gone some time before, taking her companion with her, the devotees were the same, — the two Englishmen still exchanging clean, white Bank of England notes, the German and Haytian losing, but calm as mummies, the fat, oily woman, melting like a red candle, the perspiration streaming down her face.

Suddenly I heard a convulsive gasp. The woman in black was on her feet leaning over the table. Her eyes blazed in a frenzy of delight. She was sweeping into her open hands the piles of gold before her. By some marvelous stroke of luck, and with almost her last louis, she had won every franc on the cloth!

Then she drew herself up defiantly, covered her face with her veil, hugged the money to her breast, and staggered from the room.

II

So deep an impression had the gambling scene of the night before made upon me that the next morning I loitered under the Noah's-ark trees, hoping I might identify the woman, and in some impossible, improbable way know more of her history. I even lounged into the Casino, tried the door at which I had knocked the night before, and, finding it locked and the scrubwoman suspicious, strolled out carelessly into the garden, and, sitting down under the palms, tried to pick out the windows that opened into the gaming-room. But they were all alike, with pots of flowers blooming in each.

Still burdened with these memories, I entered the church, — the old church with square towers and deep-receding entrance, that stands on the crest of a steep hill overlooking the Casino, and within a short distance of the Noah's-ark trees. Every afternoon, near the hour of twilight, when the shadows reach down Mount Pilatus, and the mists gather in the valley, a broken procession of strollers, in twos and threes and larger groups, slowly climb its path. They are on their way to hear the great organ played.

The audience was already seated. It was at the moment of that profound hush which precedes the recital. Even my footfall, light as it was, reëchoed to the groined arches. The church was ghostly dark,—so dark that the hundreds of heads melted into the mass of pews, and they into the gloom of column and wall. The only distinguishable gleam was the soft glow of the dying day struggling through the lower panes of the dust-begrimed windows. Against these hung long chains holding unlighted lamps.

I felt my way to an empty pew on a side aisle, and sat down. The silence continued. Now and again there was a slight cough, instantly checked. Once a child dropped a book, the echoes lasting apparently for minutes. The darkness became almost black night. Only the clean, new panes of glass used in repairing some break in the begrimed windows showed clear. These seemed to hang out like small square lanterns.

Suddenly I was aware that the stillness was broken by a sound faint as a sigh, delicate as the first breath of a storm. Then came a great sweep growing louder, the sweep of deep thunder tones with the roar of the tempest, the rush of the mighty rain, the fury of the avalanche, the voices of the birds singing in the sunlight, the gurgle of the brooks, and the soft cadence of the angelus calling the peasants to prayers. Then, a pause and another burst of melody, ending in profound silence, as if the door of heaven had been opened and as quickly shut. Then a clear voice springing into life, singing like a lark, rising, swelling—up—up—filling the church—the roof—the sky! Then the heavenly door thrown wide, and the melody pouring out in a torrent, drowning the voice. Then above it all, while I sat quivering, there soared like a bird in the air, singing as it flew, one great, superb, vibrating, resolute note, pure, clear, full, sensuous, untrammeled, dominating the heavens: not human, not divine; like no woman's, like no man's, like no angel's ever dreamed of,—the vox humana.

It did not awaken in me any feeling of reverence or religious ecstasy. I only remember that the music took possession of my soul. That beneath and through it all I felt the vibrations of all the tragic things that come to men and women in their lives. Scenes from out an irrelevant past swept across my mind. I heard again the long winding note of the bugle echoing through the pines, the dead in uneven rows, the moon lighting their faces. I caught once more the cry of the girl my friend loved, he who died and never knew. I saw the quick plunge of the strong swimmer, white arms clinging to his neck, and heard once more that joyous shout from a hundred throats. And I could still hear the hoarse voice of the captain with drenched book and flickering lantern, and shivered again as I caught the dull splash of the sheeted body dropping into the sea.

The vox humana stopped, not gradually, but abruptly, as if the heart had broken and its life had gone out in the one supreme effort. Then silence,—a silence so profound that a low sob from the pew across the aisle startled me. I strained my eyes, and caught the outlines of a woman heavily veiled. I could see, too, a child beside her, his head on her shoulder. The boy was bare-headed, his curls splashed over her black dress. Then another sob, half smothered, as if the woman were strangling.

No other sound broke the stillness; only the feeling everywhere of pent-up, smothered sighs.

In this intense moment a faint footfall was heard approaching from the church door, walking in the gloom. It proved to be that of an old man, bent and trembling. He came slowly down the sombre church, with unsteady, shambling gait, holding in one hand a burning taper,—a mere speck. In the other he carried a rude lantern, its wavering light hovering about his feet. As he passed in his long brown cloak, the swaying light encircled his white beard and hair with a fluffy halo. He moved slowly, the spark he carried no larger than a firefly. The sacristan had come to light the candles.

He stopped half way down the middle aisle, opposite a pew, the faint flush of his lantern falling on the nearest upturned face. A long thin candle was fastened to this pew. The firefly of a taper, held aloft in his trembling hand, flickered uncertainly like a moth, and rested on the top of this candle. Then the wick kindled and burned.

As its rays felt their way over the vast interior, struggling up into the dark roof, reaching the gilded ornaments on the side altar enshrouded in gloom, glinting on the silver of the hanging lamps, a plaintive note fluttered softly, swelled into an ecstasy of sound, and was lost in a chorus of angel voices.

The sacristan moved down the aisle, kindled two other candles on the distant altar, and was lost in the shadows.

The woman in the pew across the aisle bent forward, resting her head on the back of the seat in front, drawing the child to her. The boy cuddled closer. As she turned, a spark of light trickled down her cheek. I caught sight of the falling tear, but could not see the face.

The music ceased; the last anthem had been played; a gas-jet flared in the organ-loft; the people began to rise from their seats. The sacristan appeared again from behind the altar, and walked slowly down the side aisle, carrying only his lantern. As he neared my seat the woman stood erect, and passed out of the pew, her hand caressing the child. Surely I could not be mistaken about that movement, the slow, undulating, rhythmic walk, the floating shadow of the night before. Certainly not with the light of the sacristan's lantern now full on her face. Yes: the same finely chiseled features, the same waves of brown hair, the same eyes, the same drooping eyelids, like blossoms wet with dew! At last I had found her.

I walked behind, — so close that I could have laid my hand on her boy's head, or touched her hand as it lay buried in his curls. The old, bent sacristan stepped in front, swinging his lantern, the ghostly shadows wavering about his feet. Then he halted to let the crowd clear the main aisle.

As he stood still, the woman drew suddenly back as if stunned by a blow, clutched the boy to her side, and fixed her eyes on the lantern's ghostly shadows. I leaned over quickly. The glow of the rude lamp, with its squares of waving light flecking the stone flagging, traced in unmistakable outlines the form of a cross!

For some minutes she stood as if in a trance, her eyes fastened upon the floating shadow, her whole form trembling, bent, her body swaying. Only when the sacristan moved a few paces ahead to hold open the swinging door, and the shadow of the cross faded, did she awake from the spell.

Then, recovering herself slowly, she bowed reverently, crossed herself, drew the boy closer, and, with his hand in hers, passed out into the cool starlit night.

III

The following morning I was sitting under the Noah's-ark trees, watching the people pass and repass, when a man in a suit of white flannel, carrying a light cane, and wearing a straw hat with a red band, and a necktie to match, stopped a flower-girl immediately in front of me, and affixed an additional dot of blood-color to his buttonhole.

In the glare of the daylight he was even more yellow than when under the blaze of the gas-jets. His eyes were still glassy and brilliant, but the rims showed red, as if for want of sleep, and beneath the lower lids lay sunken half-circles of black. He moved with his wonted precision, but without that extreme gravity of manner which had characterized him the night of the game. Looked at as a mere passer-by, he would have impressed you as a rather debonair, overdressed habitué, who was enjoying his morning stroll under the trees, without other purpose in life than the breathing of the cool air and enjoyment of the attendant exercise. His spider-ship had doubtless seen me when he entered the walk,—I was still an untrapped fly,—and had picked out this particular flower-girl beside me as a safe anchorage for one end of his web. I turned away my head; but it was too late.

"Monsieur did not play last night?" the croupier asked deferentially.

"No; I did not know the game." Then an idea struck me. "Sit down; I want to talk to you." He touched the edge of his hat with one finger, opened a gold cigarette-case studded with jewels, offered me its contents, and took the seat beside me.

"Pardon the abruptness of the inquiry, but who was the woman in black?" I asked.

He looked at me curiously.

"Ah, you mean madame with the bag?"

"Yes."

"She was once the Baroness Frontignac."

"Was once! What is she now?"

"Now? Ah, that is quite a story." He stopped, shut the gold case with a click, and leaned forward, flicking the pebbles with the point of his cane. "If madame had had a larger bag she might have broken the bank. Is it not so?"

"You know her, then?" I persisted.

"Monsieur, men of my profession know everybody. Sooner or later they all come to us—when they are young, and their francs have wings; when they are gray-haired and cautious; when they are old and foolish."

"But she did not look like a gambler," I replied stiffly.

He smiled his old cynical, treacherous smile.

"Monsieur is pleased to be very pronounced in his language. A gambler! Monsieur no doubt means to say that madame has not the appearance of being under the intoxication of the play." Then with a positive tone, still flicking the pebbles, "The baroness played for love."

"Of the cards?" I asked persistently. I was determined to drive the nail to the head.

The croupier looked at me fixedly, shrugged his shoulders, laughed between his teeth, a little, hissing laugh that sounded like escaping steam, and said slowly:—

"No; of a man."

Then, noticing my increasing interest, "Monsieur would know something of madame?"

He held up his hand, and began crooking one finger after another as he recounted her history. These bent keys, it seemed, unlocked secrets as well.

"Le voilà! the drama of Madame la Baronne! The play opens when she is first a novice in the convent of Saint Ursula, devoted to good works and the church. Next you find her a grand dame and rich, the wife of Baron Alphonse de Frontignac, first secretary of legation at Vienna. Then a mother with one child, — a boy, now six or seven years old, who is hardly ever out of her arms." He stopped, toyed for a moment with his match-safe, slipped it into his pocket, and said carelessly, "So much for Act I."

Then, after a pause during which he traced again little diagrams in the gravel, he said suddenly: —

"Does this really interest you, monsieur?"

"Unquestionably."

"You know her, then?" This with a glance of suspicion as keen as it was unexpected by me.

"Never saw her in my life before," I answered frankly, "and never shall again. I leave for Paris to-day, and sail from Havre on Saturday."

He drew in the point of his cane, looked me all over with one of those comprehensive sweeps of the eye, as if he would read my inmost thought, and then, with an expression of confidence born doubtless of my evident sincerity, continued: —

"In the next act Frontignac gets mixed up in some banking scandals, — he would, like a fool, play roulette — baccarat was always his strong game, — disappears from Vienna, is arrested at the frontier, escapes, and is found the next morning under a brush-heap with a bullet through his head. This ends the search. Two years later — this is now Act III. — Madame la Baronne, without a sou to her name, is hard at work in the hospitals of Metz. The child is pensioned out near by.

"Now comes the grand romance. An officer attached to the 13th Cuirassiers — a regiment with not men enough left after Metz to muster a company — is picked up for dead, with one arm torn off, and a sabre-slash over his head, and brought to her ward. She nurses him back to life, inch by inch, and in six months he joins his regiment. Now please follow the plot. It is quite interesting. Is it not easy to see what will happen? Tender and beautiful, young and brave! Vive le bel amour! It is the old story, but it is also une affaire de cœur—la grande passion. In a few months they are married, and he takes her to his home in Rouen. There he listens to her entreaties, and resigns his commission.

"This was five years ago. To-day he is a broken-down man, starving on his pension; a poor devil about the streets, instead of a general commanding a department; and all for love of her. Some, of course, said it was the sabre-cut; some that he could no longer hold his command, he was so badly slashed. But it is as I tell you. You can see him here any day, sitting under the trees, playing with the child, or along the lake front, leaning on her arm."

Here the croupier rose from the bench, looked critically over his case of cigarettes, selected one carefully, and began buttoning his coat as if to go.

By this time I had determined to know the end. I felt that he had told me the truth as far as he had gone; but I felt, also, that he had stopped at the most critical point of her career. I saw, too, that he was familiar with its details.

"Go on, please. Here, try a cigar." My interest in my heroine had even made me courteous. My aversion to him, too, was wearing off. Perhaps, after all, croupiers were no worse than other people. "Now, one thing more. Why was she in your gambling-house?"

He lighted the cigar, touched his hat with his forefinger, and again seated himself.

"Well, then, monsieur, as you will. I always trust you Americans. When you lose, you pay; when you win, you keep your mouths shut. Besides,"—this was spoken more to himself,—"you have never seen him, and never will. Le voilà. One night,—this only a year ago, remember,—in one of the gardens at Baden, a hand touched the baroness's shoulder.

"It was *Frontignac's*.

"The body under the brush-heap had been that of another man dressed in Frontignac's clothes. The bullet-hole in his head was made by a ball from Frontignac's pistol. Since then he had been hiding in exile.

"He threatened exposure. She pleaded for her boy and her crippled husband. She could, of course, have handed him over to the nearest gendarme; but that meant arrest, and arrest meant exposure. At their home in Vienna, let me tell you, baccarat had been played nightly as a pastime for their guests. So great was her luck that 'As lucky as the Baronne Frontignac' was a byword. Frontignac's price was this: she must take his fifty louis and play that stake at the Casino that night; when she brought him ten thousand francs he would vanish.

"That night at Baden—I was dealing, and know—she won twelve thousand francs in as many minutes. Here her slavery began. It will continue until Frontignac is discovered and captured; then he will put a second bullet into his own head. When I saw her enter my room I knew he had turned up again. As she staggered out, one of my men shadowed her. I was right; Frontignac was skulking in the garden."

All my disgust for the croupier returned in an instant. He was still the same bloodless spider of the night before. I could hardly keep my hands off him.

"And you permit this, and let this woman suffer these tortures, her life made miserable by this scoundrel, when a word, even a look, from you would send him out of the country and"—

"Softly, monsieur, softly. Why blame me? What business is it of mine. Do I love the cripple? Have I robbed the bank and murdered my double? This is not my game; it is Frontignac's. Would you have me kick over his chess board?"

JONATHAN

He was so ugly,—outside, I mean: long and lank, flat-chested, shrunken, round-shouldered, stooping when he walked; body like a plank, arms and legs like split rails, feet immense, hands like paddles, head set on a neck scrawny as a picked chicken's, hair badly put on and in patches, some about his head, some around his jaws, some under his chin in a half moon,—a good deal on the back of his hands and on his chest. Nature had hewn him in the rough and had left him with every axe mark showing.

He wore big shoes tied with deer hide strings and nondescript breeches that wrinkled along his knotted legs like old gun covers. These were patched and repatched with various hues and textures,—parts of another pair,—bits of a coat and fragments of tailor's cuttings. Sewed in their seat was half of a cobbler's apron,—for greater safety in sliding over ledges and logs, he would tell you. Next came a leather belt polished with use, and then a woolen shirt,—any kind of a shirt,—cross-barred or striped,—whatever the store had cheapest, and over that a waistcoat with a cotton back and some kind of a front, looking like a state map, it had so many colored patches. There was never any coat,—none that I remember. When he wore a coat he was another kind of a Jonathan,—a store-dealing Jonathan, or a church-going Jonathan, or a town-meeting Jonathan,—not the "go-a-fishin'," or "bee-huntin'," or "deer-stalkin'" Jonathan whom I knew.

There was a wide straw hat, too, that crowned his head and canted with the wind and flopped about his neck, and would have sailed away down many a mountain brook but for a faithful leather strap that lay buried in the half-moon whiskers and held on for dear life. And from under the rim of this thatch, and half hidden in the matted masses of badly adjusted hair, was a thin, peaked nose, bridged by a pair of big spectacles, and somewhere below these, again, a pitfall of a mouth covered with twigs of hair and an underbrush of beard, while deep-set in the whole tangle, like still pools reflecting the blue and white of the sweet heavens above, lay his eyes,—eyes that won you, kindly, twinkling, merry, trustful, and trusting eyes. Beneath these pools of light, way down below, way down where his heart beat warm, lived Jonathan.

I know a fruit in Mexico, delicious in flavor, called Timburici, covered by a skin as rough and hairy as a cocoanut; and a flower that bristles with thorns before it blooms into waxen beauty; and there are agates encrusted with clay and pearls that lie hidden in oysters. All these things, somehow, remind me of Jonathan.

His cabin was the last bit of shingle and brick chimney on that side of the Franconia Notch. There were others, farther on in the forest, with bark slants for shelter, and forked sticks for swinging kettles; but civilization ended with Jonathan's store-stove and the square of oil-cloth that covered his sitting-room floor. Upstairs, under the rafters, there was a guest-chamber smelling of pine boards and drying herbs, and sheltering a bed gridironed with bed-cord and softened by a thin layer of feathers encased in a ticking and covered with a cotton quilt. This bed always made a deep impression upon me mentally and bodily. Mentally, because I always slept so soundly in it whenever I visited Jonathan,—even with the rain pattering on the roof and the wind soughing through the big pine-trees; and bodily, because—well, because of the cords. Beside this bed was a chair for my candle, and on the floor a small square plank, laid loosely over the stovepipe hole which, in winter, held the pipe.

In summer mornings Jonathan made an alarm clock of this plank, flopping it about with the end of a fishing-rod poked up from below, never stopping until he saw my sleepy face peering down into his own. There was no bureau, only a nail or so in the scantling, and no washstand, of course; the tin basin at the well outside was better.

Then there was an old wife that lived in the cabin,—an old wife made of sole leather, with yellow-white hair and a thin, pinched face and a body all angles,—chest, arms, everywhere,—outlined through her straight up and down calico dress. When she spoke, however, you stopped to listen,—it was like a wood sound, low and far away,—soft as a bird call. People living alone in the forests often have these voices.

Last there was a dog,—a mean, sniveling, stump-tailed dog, of no particular breed or kidney. One of those dogs whose ancestry went to the bad many generations before he was born. A dog part fox,— he got all his slyness here; and part wolf, this made him ravenous; and part bull-terrier, this made him ill-tempered; and all the rest poodle, that made him too lazy to move.

The wife knew this dog, and hung the bacon on a high nail out of his reach, and covered with a big dish the pies cooling on the bench; and the neighbors down the road knew him and chased him out of their dairy-cellars when he nosed into the milk-pans and cheese-pots; and even the little children found out what a coward he was, and sent him howling home to his hole under the porch, where he grumbled and pouted all day like a spoiled child that had been half whipped. Everybody knew him, and everybody despised him for a low-down, thieving, lazy cur,—everybody except Jonathan. Jonathan loved him,—loved his weepy, smeary eyes, and his rough, black hair, and his fat round body, short stumpy legs, and shorter stumpy tail,—especially the tail. Everything else that the dog lacked could be traced back to the peccadillos of his ancestors,—Jonathan was responsible for the tail.

"Ketched in a b'ar-trap I hed sot up back in thet green timber on Loon Pond Maountin' six year ago last fall, when he wuz a pup," he would say, holding the dog in his lap,—his favorite seat. "I swan, ef it warn't too bad! Thinks I, when I sot it, I'll tell the leetle cuss whar it wuz; then—I must hev forgot it. It warn't a week afore he wuz runnin' a rabbet and run right into it. Wall, sir, them iron jaws took thet tail er his'n off julluk a knife. He's allus been kinder sore ag'in me sence, and I dunno but he's right, fur it wuz mighty keerless in me. Wall, sir, he come yowlin' hum, and when he see me he did look saour,—no use talkin',—jest ez ef he wuz a-sayin', 'Yer think you're paowerful cunnin' with yer b'ar-traps, don't ye? Jest see what it's done to my tail. It's kinder sp'ilt me for a dog.' All my fault, warn't it, George?" patting his head. (Only Jonathan would call a dog George.)

Here the dog would look up out of one eye as he spoke,—he hadn't forgotten the bear-trap, and never intended to let Jonathan forget it either. Then Jonathan would admire ruefully the end of the stump, stroking the dog all the while with his big, hairy, paddle-like hands, George rooting his head under the flap of the party-colored waistcoat.

One night, I remember, we had waited supper,—the wife and I,—we were obliged to wait, the trout being in Jonathan's creel,—when Jonathan walked in, looking tired and worried.

"Hez George come home, Marthy?" he asked, resting his long bamboo rod against the porch rail and handing the creel of trout to the wife. "No? Wall, I'm beat ef thet ain't cur'us. Guess I got ter look him up." And he disappeared hurriedly into the darkening forest, his anxious, whistling call growing fainter and fainter as he was lost in its depths. Marthy was not uneasy,—not about the dog; it was the supper that troubled her. She knew Jonathan's ways, and she knew

George. This was a favorite trick of the dog's,—this of losing Jonathan.

The trout were about burnt to a crisp and the corn-bread stone cold when Jonathan came trudging back, George in his arms,—a limp, soggy, half-dead dog, apparently. Marthy said nothing. It was an old story. Half the time Jonathan carried him home.

"Supper's ready," she said quietly, and we went in.

George slid out of Jonathan's arms, smelt about for a soft plank, and fell in a heap on the porch, his chin on his paws, his mean little eyes watching lazily,—speaking to nobody, noticing nobody, sulking all to himself. There he stayed until he caught a whiff of the fragrant, pungent odor of fried trout. Then he cocked one eye and lifted an ear. He must not carry things too far. Next, I heard a single thump of his six-inch tail. George was beginning to get pleased; he always did when there were things to eat.

All this time Jonathan, tired out, sat in his big splint chair at the supper-table. He had been thrashing the brook since daylight,— over his knees sometimes. I could still see the high-water mark on his patched trousers. Another whiff of the frying-pan, and George got up. He dared not poke his nose into Marthy's lap,—there were too many chunks of wood within easy reach of her hand. So he sidled up to Jonathan, rubbing his nose against his big knees, whining hungrily, looking up into his face.

"I tell ye," said Jonathan, smiling at me, patting the dog as he spoke, "this yere George hez got more sense'n most men. He knows what's become of them trout we ketched. I guess he's gittin' over the way I treated him to-day. Ye see, we wuz up the East Branch when he run a fox south. Thinks I, the fox'll take a whirl back and cross the big runway; and, sure enough, it warn't long afore I heard George a-comin' back, yippin' along up through Hank Simons' holler. So I whistled to him and steered off up onto the maountin' to take a look at Bog-eddy and try and git a pickerel. When I come daown ag'in, I see George warn't whar I left him, so I hollered and whistled ag'in. Then, thinks I, you're mad 'cause I left ye, an' won't let on ye *kin* hear; so I come along hum without him. When I went back a while ago a-lookin' for him, would yer believe it, thar he wuz a-layin' in the road, about forty rod this side of Hank Simons' sugar maples, flat onto his stummick an' disgusted an' put out awful. It wuz about all I could do ter git him hum. I knowed the minute I come in fust time an' see he warn't here thet his feelin's wuz hurt 'cause I left him. I presaume mebbe I oughter hollered ag'in afore I got so fer off. Then I thought, of course, he knowed I'd gone to Bog-eddy. Beats all, what sense some dogs hez."

I never knew Jonathan to lose patience with George but once: that was when the dog tried to burrow into the hole of a pair of chip-munks whom Jonathan loved. They lived in a tree blanketed with moss and lying across the wood road. George had tried to scrape an acquaintance by crawling in uninvited, nearly scaring the little fel-lows to death, and Jonathan had flattened him into the dry leaves with his big, paddle-like hands. That was before the bear-trap had nipped his tail, but George never forgot it.

He was particularly polite to chipmunks after that. He would lie still by the hour and hear Jonathan talk to them without even a whine of discontent. I watched the old man one morning up be-neath the ledges, groping, on his hands and knees, filling his pock-ets with nuts, and when he reached the wood road, emptying them in a pile near the chipmunk's tree, George looking on good-naturedly.

"Guess you leetle cunnin's better hurry up," he said, while he poured out the nuts on the ground, his knees sticking up as he sat, like some huge grasshopper's. "Guess ye ain't got more 'n time to fill yer cubbud,—winter's a-comin'! Them leetle birches on Bog-eddy is turnin' yeller,—that's the fust sign. 'Fore ye knows it snow'll be fly-in'. Then whar'll ye be with everything froze tighter'n Sampson bound the heathen, you cunnin' leetle skitterin' pups. Then I presaume likely ye'll come a-drulin' raound an' want me an' George should gin ye suthin to git through th' winter on,—won't they, George?"

"Beats all," he said to me that night, "how thoughtful some dogs is. Hadn't been fer George to-day, I'd clean forgot them leetle folks. I see him scratching raound in the leaves an' I knowed right away what he wuz thinkin' of."

Often when I was sketching in the dense forest, Jonathan would lie down beside me, the old flop of a hat under his head, his talk rambling on.

"I don't wonder ye like to paint 'em. Thar hain't nothin' so human as trees. Take thet big hemlock right in front er yer. Hain't he led a pretty decent life? See how praoud an' tall he's growed, with them arms of his'n straight aout an' them leetle chillen of his'n spraouting up raound him. I tell ye them hemlocks is pretty decent people. Now take a look at them two white birches down by thet big rock. Ain't it a shame the way them fellers hez been goin' on sence they wuz leetle saplin's, makin' it so nothin' could grow raound 'em,— with their jackets all ragged an' tore like tramps, an' their toes all out of their shoes whar ther roots is stickin' clear of the bark,—ain't they a-ketchin' it in their ole age? An' then foller on daown whar thet leetle bunch er silver maples is dancin' in the sunlight, so slender an' cunnin',—all aout in their summer dresses, julluk a bevy er young gals,—ain't they human like? I tell ye, trees is the humanest things thet is."

These talks with me made George restless. He was never happy unless Jonathan had *him* on his mind.

But it was a cluster of daisies that first lifted the inner lid of Jonathan's heart for me. I was away up the side of the Notch overlooking the valley, my easel and canvas lashed to a tree, the wind blew so, when Jonathan came toiling up the slope, a precipice in fact, with a tin can strapped to his back, filled with hot corn and some doughnuts, and threw himself beside me, the sweat running down his weather-tanned neck.

"So long ez we know whar you're settin' at work it ain't nat'ral to let ye starve, be it?" throwing himself beside me. George had started ahead of him and had been picked up and carried as usual.

When Jonathan sat upright, after a breathing spell, his eye fell on a tuft of limp, bruised daisies, flattened to the earth by the heel of his clumsy shoe. There were acres of others in sight.

"Gosh hang!" he said, catching his breath suddenly, as if something had stung him, and reaching down with his horny, bent fingers, "ef thet ain't too bad." Then to himself in a tone barely audible,—he had entirely forgotten my presence,—"You never had no sense, Jonathan, nohow, stumblin' raound like er bull calf tramplin' everything. Jes' see what ye've gone an' done with them big feet er yourn," bending over the bruised plant and tenderly adjusting the leaves. "Them daisies hez got jest ez good a right ter live ez you hev."

I was almost sure when I began that I had a story to tell. I had thought of that one about Luke Pollard,—the day Luke broke his leg behind Loon Mountain, and Jonathan carried him down the gorge on his back, crossing ledges that would have scared a goat. It was snowing at the time, they said, and blowing a gale. When they got half way down White Face, Jonathan's foot slipped and he fell into the ravine, breaking his wrist. Only the drifts saved his life. Luke caught a sapling and held on. The doctor set Jonathan's wrist last, and Luke never knew it had been broken until the next day. It is one of the stories they tell you around the stove winter evenings.

"Julluk the night Jonathan carried aout Luke," they say, listening to the wind howling over the ledges.

And then I thought of that other story that Hank Simons told me,—the one about the mill back of Woodstock caving in from the freshet and burying the miller's girl. No one dared lift the timbers until Jonathan crawled in. The child was pinned down between the beams, and the water rose so fast they feared the wreckage would sweep the mill. Jonathan clung to the sills waist-deep in the torrent, crept under the floor timbers, and then bracing his back held the beam until he dragged her clear. It happened a good many years ago, but Hank always claimed it had bent Jonathan's back.

But, after all, they are not the things I love best to remember of Jonathan.

It is always the old man's voice, crooning his tuneless song as he trudges home in the twilight, his well-filled creel at his side,—the good-for-nothing dog in his arms; or it is that look of sweet contentment on his face,—the deep and thoughtful eyes, filled with the calm serenity of his soul. And then the ease and freedom of his life! Plenty of air and space, and plenty of time to breathe and move! Having nothing, possessing all things! No bonds to guard,—no cares to stifle,—no trains to catch,—no appointments to keep,—no fashions to follow,—no follies to shun! Only the old wife and worthless, lazy dog, and the rod and the creel! Only the blessed sunshine and fresh, sweet air, and the cool touch of deep woods.

No, there is no story—only Jonathan.

ALONG THE BRONX

Hidden in our memories there are quaint, quiet nooks tucked away at the end of leafy lanes; still streams overhung with feathery foliage; gray rocks lichen-covered; low-ground meadows, knee-deep in lush grass; restful, lazy lakes dotted with pond-lilies; great, wide-spreading trees, their arms uplifted in song, their leaves quivering with the melody.

I say there are all these delights of leaf, moss, ripple, and shade stored away somewhere in our memories,—dry bulbs of a preceding summer's bloom, that need only the first touch of spring, the first glorious day in June, to break out into flower. When they do break out, they are generally chilled in the blooming by the thousand and one difficulties of prolonged travel, time of getting there and time of getting back again, expense, and lack of accommodations.

If you live in New York—and really you should not live anywhere else!—there are a few buttons a tired man can touch that will revive for him all these delights in half an hour's walk, costing but a car-fare, and robbing no man or woman of time, even without the benefits of the eight-hour law.

You touch one of these buttons when you plan to spend an afternoon along the Bronx.

There are other buttons, of course. You can call up the edges of the Palisades, with their great sweep of river below, the seething, steaming city beyond; or, you can say "Hello!" to the Upper Harlem, with its house-boats and floating restaurants; or you can ring up Westchester and its picturesque waterline. But you cannot get them all together in half an hour except in one place, and that is along the Bronx.

The Bronx is the forgotten, the overlooked, the "disremembered," as the provincial puts it. Somebody may know where it begins—I do not. I only know where it ends. What its early life may be, away up near White Plains, what farms it waters, what dairies it cools, what herds it refreshes, I know not. I only know that when I get off at Woodlawn—that City of the Silent—it comes down from somewhere up above the railroad station, and that it "takes a header," as the boys say, under an old mill, abandoned long since, and then, like another idler, goes singing along through open meadows, and around big trees in clumps, their roots washed bare, and then over sandy stretches reflecting the flurries of yellow butterflies, and then around a great hill, and so on down to Laguerre's.

Of course, when it gets to Laguerre's I know all about it. I know the old rotting landing-wharf where Monsieur moors his boats,—the one with the little seat is still there; and Lucette's big eyes are just as brown, and her hair just as black, and her stockings and slippers just as dainty on Sundays as when first I knew her. And the wooden bench is still there, where the lovers used to sit; only Monsieur, her father, tells me that François works very late in the big city,—three mouths to feed now, you see,—and only when le petit François is tucked away in his crib in the long summer nights, and Lucette has washed the dishes and put on her best apron, and the Bronx stops still in a quiet pool to listen, is the bench used as in the old time when Monsieur discovered the lovers by the flash of his lantern.

Then I know where it floats along below Laguerre's, and pulls itself together in a very dignified way as it sails under the brand-new bridge,—the old one, propped up on poles, has long since paid tribute to a spring freshet,—and quickens its pace below the old Dye-house,—also a wreck now (they say it is haunted),—and then goes slopping along in and out of the marshes, sousing the sunken willow roots, oozing through beds of weeds and tangled vines.

But only a very little while ago did I know where it began to leave off all its idle ways and took really to the serious side of life; when it began rushing down long, stony ravines, plunging over respectable, well-to-do masonry dams, skirting once costly villas, whispering between dark defiles of rock, and otherwise disporting itself as becomes a well-ordered, conventional, self-respecting mountain stream, uncontaminated by the encroachments and frivolities of civilized life.

All this begins at Fordham. Not exactly at Fordham, for you must walk due east from the station for half a mile, climb a fence, and strike through the woods before you hear its voice and catch the gleam of its tumbling current.

They will all be there when you go—all the quaint nooks, all the delights of leaf, moss, ripple, and shade, of your early memories. And in the half-hour, too,—less if you are quick-footed,—from your desk or shop in the great city.

No, you never heard of it. I knew that before you said a word. You thought it was the dumping-ground of half the cast-off tinware of the earth; that only the shanty, the hen-coop, and the stable over-hung its sluggish waters, and only the carpet shaker, the sod gath-erer, and the tramp infested its banks.

I tell you that in all my wanderings in search of the picturesque, nothing within a day's journey is half as charming. That its stretches of meadow, willow clumps, and tangled densities are as lovely, fresh, and enticing as can be found—yes, within a thousand miles of your door. That the rocks are encrusted with the thickest of moss and lichen, gray, green, black, and brilliant emerald. That the trees are superb, the solitude and rest complete. That it is finer, more subtle, more exquisite than its sister brooks in the denser forest, because that here and there it shows the trace of some human touch,—and nature is never truly picturesque without it,—the bro-ken-down fence, the sagging bridge, and vine-covered roof.

But you must go *now*.

Now, before the grip of the great city has been fastened upon it; before the axe of the "dago" clears out the wilderness of underbrush; before the landscape gardener, the sanitary engineer, and the con-tractor pounce upon it and strangle it; before the crimes of the cast-iron fountain, the varnished grapevine arbor, with seats to match, the bronze statues presented by admiring groups of citizens, the rambles, malls, and cement-lined caverns, are consummated; before the gravel walk confines your steps, and the granite curbing impris-ons the flowers, as if they, too, would escape.

Now, when the tree lies as it falls; when the violets bloom and are there for the picking; when the dogwood sprinkles the bare branches with white stars, and the scent of the laurel fills the air.

Touch the button some day soon for an hour along the Bronx.

ANOTHER DOG

Do not tell me dogs cannot talk. I know better. I saw it all myself. It was at Sterzing, that most picturesque of all the Tyrolean villages on the Italian slope of the Brenner, with its long, single street, zigzagged like a straggling path in the snow,—perhaps it was laid out in that way,—and its little open square, with shrine and rude stone fountain, surrounded by women in short skirts and hobnailed shoes, dipping their buckets. On both sides of this street ran queer arcades sheltering shops, their doorways piled with cheap stuffs, fruit, farm implements, and the like, and at the far end, it was almost the last house in the town, stood the old inn, where you breakfast. Such an old, old inn! with swinging sign framed by fantastic iron work, and decorated with overflows of foaming ale in green mugs, crossed clay pipes, and little round dabs of yellow-brown cakes. There was a great archway, too, wide and high, with enormous, barn-like doors fronting on this straggling, zigzag, sabot-trodden street. Under this a cobble-stone pavement led to the door of the coffee-room and out to the stable beyond. These barn-like doors keep out the driving snows and the whirls of sleet and rain, and are slammed to behind horse, sleigh, and all, if not in the face, certainly in the very teeth of the winter gale, while the traveler disentangles his half-frozen legs at his leisure, almost within sight of the blazing fire of the coffee-room within.

Under this great archway, then, against one of these doors, his big paws just inside the shadow line,—for it was not winter, but a brilliant summer morning, the grass all dusted with powdered diamonds, the sky a turquoise, the air a joy,—under this archway, I say, sat a big St. Bernard dog, squat on his haunches, his head well up, like a grenadier on guard. His eyes commanded the approaches down the road, up the road, and across the street; taking in the passing peddler with the tinware, and the girl with a basket strapped to her back, her fingers knitting for dear life, not to mention so unimportant an object as myself swinging down the road, my iron-shod alpenstock hammering the cobbles.

He made no objection to my entering, neither did he receive me with any show of welcome. There was no bounding forward, no wagging of the tail, no aimless walking around for a moment, and settling down in another spot; nor was there any sudden growl or forbidding look in the eye. None of these things occurred to him, for none of these things was part of his duty. The landlord would do the welcoming, the blue-shirted porter take my knapsack and show me the way to the coffee-room. His business was to sit still and guard that archway. Paying guests, and those known to the family,—yes! But stray mountain goats, chickens, inquisitive, pushing peddlers, pigs, and wandering dogs,—well, he would look out for these.

While the cutlets and coffee were being fried and boiled, I dragged a chair across the road and tilted it back out of the sun against the wall of a house. I, too, commanded a view down past the blacksmith shop, where they were heating a huge iron tire to clap on the hind wheel of a diligence, and up the street as far as the little square where the women were still clattering about on the cobbles, their buckets on their shoulders. This is how I happened to be watching the dog.

The more I looked at him, the more strongly did his personality impress me. The exceeding gravity of his demeanor! The dignified attitude! The quiet, silent reserve! The way he looked at you from under his eyebrows, not eagerly, nor furtively, but with a self-possessed, competent air, quite like a captain of a Cunarder scanning a horizon from the bridge, or a French gendarme, watching the shifting crowds from one of the little stone circles anchored out in the rush of the boulevards,—a look of authority backed by a sense of unlimited power. Then, too, there was such a dignified cut to his hairy chops as they drooped over his teeth beneath his black, stubby nose. His ears rose and fell easily, without undue haste or excitement when the sound of horses' hoofs put him on his guard, or a goat wandered too near. Yet one could see that he was not a meddlesome dog, nor a snarler, no running out and giving tongue at each passing object, not that kind of a dog at all! He was just a plain, substantial, well-mannered, dignified, self-respecting St. Bernard dog, who knew his place and kept it, who knew his duty and did it, and who would no more chase a cat than he would bite your legs in the dark. Put a cap with a gold band on his head and he would really have made an ideal concierge. Even without the band, he concentrated in his person all the superiority, the repose, and exasperating reticence of that necessary concomitant of Continental hotel life.

Suddenly I noticed a more eager expression on his face. One ear was unfurled, like a flag, and almost run to the masthead; the head was turned quickly down the road. A sound of wheels was heard below the shop. His dogship straightened himself and stood on four legs, his tail wagging slowly.

Another dog was coming.

A great Danish hound, with white eyes, black-and-tan ears, and tail as long and smooth as a policeman's night-club;—one of those sleek and shining dogs with powerful chest and knotted legs, a little bowed in front, black lips, and dazzling, fang-like teeth. He was spattered with brown spots, and sported a single white foot. Altogether, he was a dog of quality, of ancestry, of a certain position in his own land,—one who had clearly followed his master's mountain wagon to-day as much for love of adventure as anything else. A dog of parts, too, who could perhaps, hunt the wild boar, or give chase to the agile deer. He was certainly not an inn dog. He was rather a palace dog, a chateau, or a shooting-box dog, who, in his off moments, trotted behind hunting carts filled with guns, sportsmen in knee-breeches, or in front of landaus when my lady went an-airing.

And with all this, and quite naturally, he was a dog of breeding, who, while he insisted on his own rights, respected those of others. I saw this before he had spoken ten words to the concierge,—the St. Bernard dog, I mean. For he did talk to him, and the conversation was just as plain to me, tilted back against the wall, out of the sun, waiting for my cutlets and coffee, as if I had been a dog myself, and understood each word of it.

First, he walked up sideways, his tail wagging and straight out, like a patent towel-rack. Then he walked round the concierge, who followed his movements with becoming interest, wagging his own tail, straightening his forelegs, and sidling around him kindly, as befitted the stranger's rank and quality, but with a certain dog-independence of manner, preserving his own dignities while courteously passing the time of day, and intimating, by certain twists of his tail, that he felt quite sure his excellency would like the air and scenery the farther he got up the pass, — all strange dogs did.

During this interchange of canine civilities, the landlord was helping out the two men, the companions of the dog. One was round and pudgy, the other lank and scrawny. Both were in knickerbockers, with green hats decorated with cock feathers and edelweiss. The blue-shirted porter carried in the bags and alpenstocks, closing the coffee-room door behind them.

Suddenly the strange dog, who had been beguiled by the courteous manner of the concierge, realized that his master had disappeared. The man had been hungry, no doubt, and half blinded by the glare of the sun. After the manner of his kind, he had dived into this shelter without a word to the dumb beast who had tramped behind his wheels, swallowing the dust his horses kicked up.

When the strange dog realized this, — I saw the instant the idea entered his mind, as I caught the sudden toss of the head, — he glanced quickly about with that uneasy, anxious look that comes into the face of a dog when he discovers that he is adrift in a strange place without his master. What other face is so utterly miserable, and what eyes so pleading, the tears just under the lids, as the lost dog's?

Then it was beautiful to see the St. Bernard. With a sudden twist of the head he reassured the strange dog, — telling him, as plainly as could be, not to worry, the gentlemen were only inside, and would be out after breakfast. There was no mistaking what he said. It was done with a peculiar curving of the neck, a reassuring wag of the tail, a glance toward the coffee-room, and a few frolicsome, kittenish jumps, these last plainly indicating that as for himself the occasion was one of great hilarity, with absolutely no cause in it for anxiety. Then, if you could have seen that anxious look fade away from the face of the strange dog, the responsive, reciprocal wag of the night-club of a tail. If you could have caught the sudden peace that came into his eyes, and have seen him as he followed the concierge to the doorway, dropping his ears, and throwing himself beside him, looking up into his face, his tongue out, panting after the habit of his race, the white saliva dropping upon his paws.

Then followed a long talk, conducted in side glances, and punctuated with the quiet laughs of more slappings of tails on the cobbles, as the concierge listened to the adventures of the stranger, or matched them with funny experiences of his own.

Here a whistle from the coffee-room window startled them. Even so rude a being as a man is sometimes mindful of his dog. In an instant both concierge and stranger were on their feet, the concierge ready for whatever would turn up, the stranger trying to locate the sound and his master. Another whistle, and he was off, bounding down the road, looking wistfully at the windows, and rushing back bewildered. Suddenly it came to him that the short cut to his master lay through the archway.

Just here there was a change in the manner of the concierge. It was not gruff, nor savage, nor severe,—it was only firm and decided. With his tail still wagging, showing his kindness and willingness to oblige, but with spine rigid and hair bristling, he explained clearly and succinctly to that strange dog how absolutely impossible it would be for him to permit his crossing the archway. Up went the spine of the stranger, and out went his tail like a bar of steel, the feet braced, and the whole body taut as standing rigging. But the concierge kept on wagging his tail, though his hair still bristled,—saying as plainly as he could:—

"My dear sir, do not blame me. I assure you that nothing in the world would give me more pleasure than to throw the whole house open to you; but consider for a moment. My master puts me here to see that nobody enters the inn but those whom he wishes to see, and that all other live-stock, especially dogs, shall on no account be admitted." (This with head bent on one side and neck arched.) "Now, while I have the most distinguished consideration for your dogship" (tail wagging violently), "and would gladly oblige you, you must see that my honor is at stake" (spine more rigid), "and I feel assured that under the circumstances you will not press a request (low growl) which you must know would be impossible for me to grant."

And the strange dog, gentleman as he was, expressed himself as entirely satisfied with the very free and generous explanation. With tail wagging more violently than ever, he assured the concierge that he understood his position exactly. Then wheeling suddenly, he bounded down the road. Though convinced, he was still anxious.

Then the concierge gravely settled himself once more on his haunches in his customary place, his eyes commanding the view up and down and across the road, where I sat still tilted back in my chair waiting for my cutlets, his whole body at rest, his face expressive of that quiet content which comes from a sense of duties performed and honor untarnished.

But the stranger had duties, too; he must answer the whistle, and find his master. His search down the road being fruitless, he rushed back to the concierge, looking up into his face, his eyes restless and anxious.

"If it were inconsistent with his honor to permit him to cross the threshold, was there any other way he could get into the coffee-room?" This last with a low whine of uneasiness, and a toss of head.

"Yes, certainly," jumping to his feet, "why had he not mentioned it before? It would give him very great pleasure to show him the way to the side entrance." And the St. Bernard, everything wagging now, walked with the stranger to the corner, stopping stock still to point with his nose to the closed door.

Then the stranger bounded down with a scurry and plunge, nervously edging up to the door, wagging his tail, and with a low, anxious whine springing one side and another, his paws now on the sill, his nose at the crack, until the door was finally opened, and he dashed inside.

What happened in the coffee-room I do not know, for I could not see. I am willing, however, to wager that a dog of his loyalty, dignity, and sense of duty did just what a dog of quality would do. No awkward springing at his master's chest with his dusty paws leaving marks on his vest front; no rushing around chairs and tables in mad joy at being let in, alarming waitresses and children. Only a low whine and gurgle of delight, a rubbing of his cold nose against his master's hand, a low, earnest look up into his face, so frank, so trustful, a look that carried no reproach for being shut out, and only gratitude for being let in.

A moment more, and he was outside again, head in air, looking for his friend. Then a dash, and he was around by the archway, licking the concierge in the face, biting his neck, rubbing his nose under his forelegs, saying over and over again how deeply he thanked him, — how glad and proud he was of his acquaintance, and how delighted he would be if he came down to Vienna, or Milan, or wherever he did come from, so that he might return his courtesies in some way, and make his stay pleasant.

Just here the landlord called out that the cutlets and coffee were ready, and, man-like, I went in to breakfast.

BROCKWAY'S HULK

I first saw Brockway's towards the close of a cold October day. Since early morning I had been tramping and sketching about the northern suburbs of New York, and it was late in the afternoon when I reached the edge of that high ground overlooking the two rivers. I could see through an opening in the woods the outline of the great aqueduct, — a huge stone centipede stepping across on its sturdy legs; the broad Hudson, with its sheer walls of rock, and the busy Harlem crowded with boats and braced with bridges. A raw wind was blowing, and a gray mist blurred the edges of the Palisades where they cut against the sky.

As the darkness fell the wind increased, and scattered drops of rain, piloting the coming storm, warned me to seek a shelter. Shouldering my trap and hurrying forward, I descended the hill, followed the road to the East River, and, finding no boat, walked along the shore hoping to hail a fisherman or some belated oarsman, and reach the station opposite.

My search led me around a secluded cove edged with white sand and yellow marsh grass, ending in a low, jutting point. Here I came upon a curious sort of dwelling, — half house, half boat. It might have passed for an abandoned barge, or wharf boat, too rotten to float and too worthless to break up, — the relic and record of some by-gone tide of phenomenal height. When I approached nearer it proved to be an old-fashioned canal-boat, sunk to the water line in the grass, its deck covered by a low-hipped roof. Midway its length was cut a small door, opening upon a short staging or portico which supported one end of a narrow, rambling bridge leading to the shore. This bridge was built of driftwood propped up on shad poles. Over the door itself flapped a scrap of a tattered sail which served as an awning. Some pots of belated flowers bloomed on the sills of the ill-shaped windows, and a wind-beaten vine, rooted in a fish basket, crowded into the door, as if to escape the coming winter. Nothing could have been more dilapidated or more picturesque.

The only outward sign of life about the dwelling was a curl of blue smoke. Without this signal of good cheer it had a menacing look, as it lay in its bed of mud glaring at me from under its eaves of eyebrows, shading eyes of windows a-glint in the fading light.

I crossed the small beach strewn with oyster shells, ascended the tottering bridge, and knocked. The door was opened by a gray-bearded old man in a rough jacket. He was bare-footed, his trousers rolled up above his ankles, like a boy's.

"Can you help me across the river?" I asked.

"Yes, perhaps I can. Come into the Hulk," he replied, holding the door against the gusts of wind.

The room was small and low, with doors leading into two others. In its centre, before a square stove, stood a young child cooking the evening meal. I saw no other inmates.

"You are wet," said the old man, laying his hand on my shoulder, feeling me over carefully; "come nearer the stove."

The child brought a chair. As I dropped into it I caught his eye fixed upon me intently.

"What are you?" he said abruptly, noting my glance,—"a peddler." He said this standing over me,—his arms akimbo, his bare feet spread apart.

"No, a painter," I answered smiling; my trap had evidently misled him.

He mused a little, rubbing his beard with his thumb and forefinger; then, making a mental inventory of my exterior, beginning with my slouch hat and taking in each article down to my tramping shoes, he said slowly, —

"And poor?"

"Yes, we all are." And I laughed; his manner made me a little uncomfortable.

My reply, however, seemed to reassure him. His features relaxed and a more kindly expression overspread his countenance.

"And now, what are *you*?" I asked, offering him a cigarette as I spoke.

"Me? Nothing," he replied curtly, refusing it with a wave of his hand. "Only Brockway, —just Brockway, —that's all, —just Brockway." He kept repeating this in an abstracted way, as if the remark was addressed to himself, the words dying in his throat.

Then he moved to the door, took down an oilskin from a peg, and saying that he would get the boat ready, went out into the night, shutting the door behind him, his bare feet flapping like wet fish as he walked.

I was not sorry I was going away so soon. The man and the place seemed uncanny.

I roused myself and crossed the room, attracted by the contents of a cupboard filled with cheap pottery and some bits of fine old English lustre. Then I examined the furniture of the curious interior, — the high-backed chairs, mahogany table, —one leg replaced with pine, —the hair sofa and tall clock in the corner by the door. They were all old and once costly, and all of a pattern of by-gone days. Everything was scrupulously clean, even to the strip of unbleached muslin hung at the small windows.

The door blew in with a whirl of wind, and Brockway entered shaking the wet from his sou'wester.

"You must wait," he said. "Dan the brakeman has taken my boat to the Railroad Dock. He will return in an hour. If you are hungry, you can sup with us. Emily, set a place for the painter."

His manner was more frank. He seemed less uncanny too. Perhaps he had been in some special ill humor when I entered. Perhaps, too, he had been suspicious of me; I had not thought of that before.

The child spread the cloth and busied herself with the dishes and plates. She was about twelve years old, slightly built and neatly dressed. Her eyes were singularly large and expressive. The light brown hair about her shoulders held a tinge of gold when the lamplight shone upon it.

Despite the evident poverty of the interior, a certain air of refinement pervaded everything. Even the old man's bare feet did not detract from it. These, by the way, he never referred to; it was evidently a habit with him. I felt this refinement not only in the relics of what seemed to denote better days, but in the arrangement of the table, the placing of the tea tray and the providing of a separate pot for the hot water. Their voices, too, were low, characteristic of people who live alone and in peace, — especially the old man's.

Brockway resumed his seat and continued talking, asking about the city as if it were a thousand miles away instead of being almost at his door; of the artists, — their mode of life, their successes, etc. As he talked his eye brightened and his manner became more gentle. It was only his outside that seemed to belong to an old boatman, roughened by the open air, with hands hard and brown. Yet these were well shaped, with tapering fingers. One bore a gold ring curiously marked and worn to a thread.

I asked about the fishing, hoping the subject would lead him to talk of his own life, and so solve the doubt in my mind as to his class and antecedents. His replies showed his thorough knowledge of his trade. He deplored the scarcity of bass, now that the steamboats and factories fouled the river; the decrease of the oysters, of which he had several beds, all being injured by the same cause. Then he broke out against the encroachments of the real estate pirates, as he called them, staking out lots behind the Hulk and destroying his privacy.

"But you own the marsh?" I asked carelessly. I saw instantly in his face the change working in his mind. He looked at me searchingly, almost fiercely, and said, weighing each word, —

"Not one foot, young man,—do you hear?—not one foot! Own nothing but what you see. But this hulk is mine,—mine from the mud to the ridgepole, with every rotten timber in it."

The outburst was so sudden that I rose from my chair. For a moment he seemed consumed with an inward rage,—not directed to me in any way,—more as if the memory of some past wrong had angered him.

Here the child, with an anxious face, rose quickly from her seat by the window, and laid her hand on his.

The old man looked into her face for a moment, and then, as if her touch had softened him, rose courteously, took her arm, seated her at the table and then me. In a moment more he had regained his gentle manner.

The meal was a frugal one, broiled fish and potatoes, a loaf of bread, and stewed apples served in a cut glass dish with broken handles.

The meal over, the girl replaced the cotton cloth with a red one, retrimmed the lamps, and disappeared into an adjoining room, carrying the dishes. The old man lighted his pipe and seated himself in a large chair, smoking on in silence. I opened my portfolio and began retouching the sketches of the morning.

Outside the weather grew more boisterous. The wind increased; the rain thrashed against the small windows, the leakage dropping on the floor like the slow ticking of a clock.

As the evening wore on I began to be uneasy, speculating as to the possibility of my reaching home that night. To be entirely frank, I did not altogether like my surroundings or my host. One moment he was like a child; the next there came into his face an expression of uncontrollable hate that sent a shiver through me. But for the clear, steady gaze of his eye I should have doubted his sanity.

There was no sign of the return of the boat. The old man became restless himself. He said nothing, but every now and then he would peer through the window and raise his hand to his ear as if listening. It was evident that he did not want me over night if he could help it. This partly reassured me.

Finally, he laid down his pipe, put on his oilskin again, lighted a lantern, and pulled the door behind him, the wind struggling to force an entrance.

In a few minutes he returned with lantern out, the rain glistening on his white, bushy beard. Without a word, he hung up his dripping garments, placed the lantern on the floor, and called the child into the adjoining room. When he came back, he laid his hand on my shoulder and said, with a tone in his voice that was unmistakable in its sincerity:—

"I am sorry, friend, but the boat cannot get back to-night. You seem like a decent man, and I believe you are. I knew some of your kind once, and I always liked them. You must stay where you are to-night, and have Emily's room."

I thanked him, but hoped the weather would clear. As to taking Emily's room, this I could not do. I would not, of course, disturb the child. If there was no chance of my getting away, I said, I preferred taking the floor, with my trap for a pillow. But he would not hear of it. He was not accustomed, he said, to have people stay with him, especially of late years; but when they did, they could not sleep on the floor.

The child's room proved to be the old cabin of the canal-boat, with the three steps leading down from the decks. The little slanting windows were still there, and so were the bunks,—or, rather, the lower one. The upper one had been altered into a sort of closet. On one side hung a row of shelves on which were such small knick-knacks as a child always loves,—a Christmas card or two, some books, a pin-cushion backed with shells, a doll's bonnet, besides some trinkets and strings of beads. Next to this ran a row of hooks covered by a curtain of cheap calico, half concealing her few simple dresses, with her muddy little shoes and frayed straw hat in the farther corner.

Above the head-board hung the likeness of a woman with large eyes, her hair pushed back from a wide, high forehead. It was framed in an old-fashioned black frame with a gold mat. Not a beautiful face, but so interesting and so expressive that I looked at it half a dozen times before I could return it to its place.

Everything was as clean and fresh as care could make it. When I dropped to sleep, the tide was swashing the floor beneath me, the rain still sousing and drenching the little windows and the roof.

The following week, one crisp, fresh morning, I was again at the Hulk. My experience the night of the storm had given me more confidence in Brockway, although the mystery of his life was still impenetrable. As I rounded the point, the old man and little Emily were just pushing off in the boat. He was on his way to his oyster beds a short distance off, his grappling-tongs and basket beside him. In his quick, almost gruff way, he welcomed me heartily and insisted on my staying to dinner. He would be back in an hour with a mess of oysters to help out. "Somebody has been raking my beds and I must look after them," he called to me as he rowed away.

I drew my own boat well up on the gravel, out of reach of the making tide, and put my easel close to the water's edge. I wanted to paint the Hulk and the river with the bluffs beyond. Before I had blocked in my sky, I caught sight of Brockway rowing hurriedly back, followed by a shell holding half a dozen oarsmen from one of the boating clubs down the river. The crew were out for a spin in their striped shirts and caps; the coxswain was calling to him, but he made no reply.

"Say, Mr. Brockway! will you please fill our water-keg? We have come off from the boat-house without a drop," I heard one call out.

"No; not to save your lives, I wouldn't!" he shouted back, his boat striking the beach. Springing out and catching Emily by the shoulder, pushing her before him, — "Go into the Hulk, child." Then, lowering his voice to me, "They are all alike, d—- them, all alike. Just such a gang! I know 'em, I know 'em. Get you a drink? I'll see you dead first, d—- you. See you dead first; do you hear?"

His face was livid, his eyes blazing with anger. The crew turned and shot up the river, grumbling as they went. Brockway unloaded his boat, clutching the tongs as if they were weapons; then, tying the painter to a stake, sat down and watched me at work. Soon Emily crept back and slipped one hand around her grandfather's neck.

"Do you think you can ever do that, little Frowsy-head?" he said, pointing to my sketch. I looked up. His face was as serene and sunny as that of the child beside him.

Gradually I came to know these people better. I never could tell why, our tastes being so dissimilar. I fancied, sometimes, from a remark the old man once made, that he had perhaps known some one who had been a painter, and that I reminded him of his friend, and on that account he trusted me; for I often detected him examining my brushes, spreading the bristles on his palm, or holding them to the light with a critical air. I could see, too, that their touch was not new to him.

As for me, the picturesqueness of the Hulk, the simple mode of life of the inmates, their innate refinement, the unselfish devotion of little Emily to the old man, the conflicting elements in his character, his fierceness — almost brutality — at times, his extreme gentleness at others, his rough treatment of every stranger who attempted to land on his shore, his tenderness over the child, all combined to pique my curiosity to know something of his earlier life.

Moreover, I constantly saw new beauties in the old Hulk. It always seemed to adapt itself to the changing moods of the weather, — being grave or gay as the skies lowered or smiled. In the dull November days, when the clouds drifted in straight lines of slaty gray, it assumed a weird, forbidding look. When the wind blew a gale from the northeast, and the back water of the river overflowed the marsh, — submerging the withered grass and breaking high upon the foot-bridge, — it seemed for all the world like the original tenement of old Noah himself, derelict ever since his disembarkation, and stranded here after centuries of buffetings. On other days it had a sullen air, settling back in its bed of mud as if tired out with all these miseries, glaring at you with its one eye of a window aflame with the setting sun.

As the autumn lost itself in the winter, I continued my excursions to the Hulk, sketching in the neighborhood, gathering nuts with little Emily, or helping the old man with his nets.

On one of these days a woman, plainly but neatly dressed, met me at the edge of the wood, inquired if I had seen a child pass my way, and quickly disappeared in the bushes. I noticed her anxious face and the pathos of her eyes when I answered. Then the incident passed out of my mind. A few days later I saw her again, sitting on a pile of stones as if waiting for some one. Little Emily had seen her too, and stopped to talk to her. I could follow their movements over my easel. As soon as the child caught my eye she started up and ran towards the Hulk, the woman darting again into the bushes. When I questioned Emily about it she hesitated, and said it was a poor woman who had lost her little girl and who was very sad.

Brockway himself became more and more a mystery. I sought every opportunity to coax from him something of his earlier life, but he never referred to it but once, and then in a way that left the subject more impenetrable than ever.

I was speaking of a recent trip abroad, when he turned abruptly and said: —

"Is the Milo still in that little room in the Louvre?"

"Yes," I answered, surprised.

"I am glad of that. Against that red curtain she is the most beautiful thing I know."

"When did you see the Venus?" I asked, as quietly as my astonishment would allow.

"Oh, some years ago, when I was abroad."

He was bending over and putting some new teeth in his oyster tongs at the time, riveting them on a flat-iron with a small hammer.

I agreed with him and asked carelessly what year that was and what he was doing in Paris, but he affected not to hear me and went on with his hammering, remarking that the oysters were running so small that some slipped through his tongs and he was getting too old to rake for them twice. It was only a glimpse of some part of his past, but it was all I could get. He never referred to it again.

December of that year was unusually severe. The snow fell early and the river was closed before Christmas. This shut off all communication with the Brockways except by the roundabout way I had first followed, over the hills from the west. So my weekly tramps ceased.

Late in the following February I heard, through Dan the brakeman, that the old man was greatly broken and had not been out of the Hulk for weeks. I started at once to see him. The ice was adrift and running with the tide, and the passage across was made doubly difficult by the floating cakes shelved one upon the other. When I reached the Hulk, the only sign of life was the thin curl of smoke from the rusty pipe. Even the snow of the night before lay unbroken on the bridge, showing that no foot had crossed it that morning. I knocked, and Emily opened the door.

"Oh, it's the painter, grandpa! We thought it might be the doctor."

He was sitting in an armchair by the fire, wrapped in a blanket. Holding out his hand, he motioned to a chair and said feebly: —

"How did you hear?"

"The brakeman told me."

"Yes, Dan knows. He comes over Sundays."

He was greatly changed, — his skin drawn and shrunken, — his grizzled beard, once so great a contrast to his ruddy skin, only added to the pallor of his face. He had had a slight "stroke," he thought. It had passed off, but left him very weak.

I sat down and, to change the current of his thoughts, told him of the river outside, and the shelving ice, of my life since I had seen him, and whatever I thought would interest him. He made no reply, except in monosyllables, his head buried in his hands. Soon the afternoon light faded, and I rose to go. Then he roused himself, threw the blanket from his shoulders and said in something of his old voice: —

"Don't leave me. Do you hear? Don't leave me!" this was with an authoritative gesture. Then, his voice faltering and with almost a tender tone, "Please help me through this. My strength is almost gone."

Later, when the night closed in, he called Emily to him, pushed her hair back and, kissing her forehead, said: —

"Now go to bed, little Frowsy-head. The painter will stay with me."

I filled his pipe, threw some dry driftwood in the stove, and drew my chair nearer. He tried to smoke for a moment, but laid his pipe down. For some minutes he kept his eyes on the crackling wood; then, reaching his hand out, laid it on my arm and said slowly:—

"If it were not for the child, I would be glad that the end was near."

"Has she no one to care for her?" I asked.

"Only her mother. When I am gone, she will come."

"Her mother? Why, Brockway! I did not know Emily's mother was alive. Why not send for her now," I said, looking into his shrunken face. "You need a woman's care at once."

His grasp tightened on my arm as he half rose from the chair, his eyes blazing as I had seen them that morning when he cursed the boat's crew.

"But not that woman! Never, while I live!" and he bent down his eyes on mine. "Look at me. Men sometimes cut you to the quick, and now and then a woman can leave a scar that never heals; but your own child,—do you hear?—your little girl, the only one you ever had, the one you laid store by and loved and dreamed dreams of,—*she can tear your heart out*. That's what Emily's mother did for me. Oh, a fine gentleman, with his yachts, and boats, and horses,—a fine young aristocrat! He was a thief, I tell you, a blackguard, a beast, to steal my girl. Damn him! Damn him! Damn him!" and he fell back in his chair exhausted.

"Where is she now?" I asked cautiously, trying to change his thoughts. I was afraid of the result if the outburst continued.

"God knows! Somewhere in the city. She comes here every now and then," in a weaker voice. "Emily meets her and they go off together when I am out raking my beds. Not long ago I met her outside on the foot-bridge; she did not look up; her hair is gray now, and her face is thin and old, and so sad,—not as it once was. God forgive me,—not as it once was!" He leaned forward, his face buried in his hands.

Then he staggered to his feet, took the lamp from the table, and brought me the picture I had seen in Emily's room the night of the storm.

"You can see what she was like. It was taken the year before his death and came with Emily's clothes. She found it in her box."

I held it to the light. The large, dreamy eyes seemed even more pleading than when I first had seen the picture; and the smooth hair pushed back from the high forehead, I now saw, marked all the more clearly the lines of anxious care which were then beginning to creep over the sweet young face. It seemed to speak to me in an earnest, pleading way, as if for help.

"She is your daughter, Brockway, don't forget that."

He made no reply. After a pause, I went on, "And a girl's heart is not her own. Was it all her fault?"

He pushed his chair back and stood erect, one hand raised above the other, clutching the blanket around his throat, the end trailing on the floor. By the flickering light of the dying fire he looked like some gaunt spectre towering above me, the blackness of the shadows only intensifying the whiteness of his face.

"Go on, go on. I know what you would say. You would have me wipe out the past and forget. Forget the home she ruined and the dead mother's heart she broke. Forget the weary months abroad, the tramping of London's streets looking into every woman's face, afraid it was she. Forget these years of exile and poverty, living here in this hulk like a dog, my very name unknown. When I am dead, they will say I have been cruel to her. God knows, perhaps I have; listen!" Then, glancing cautiously towards Emily's room and lowering his voice, he stooped down, his white sunken face close to mine, his eyes burning, gazed long and steadily into my face as if reading my very thoughts, and then, gathering himself up, said slowly: "No, no. I will not Let it all be buried with me. I cannot,—cannot!" and sank into his chair.

After a while he raised his head, picked up the portrait from the table and looked into its eyes eagerly, holding it in both hands; and muttering to himself, crossed the room, and threw himself on his bed. I stirred the fire, wrapped my coat about me and fell asleep on the lounge. Later, I awoke and crept into his room. He was lying on his back, the picture still clasped in his hands.

A week later, I reached the landing opposite the Hulk. There I met Dan's wife. Dan himself had been away for several days. She told me that two nights before she had been roused by a woman who had come up on the night express and wanted to be rowed over to the Hulk at once. She was in great distress, and did not mind the danger. Dan was against taking her, the ice being heavy and the night dark; but she begged so hard he had not the heart to refuse her. She seemed to be expected, for Emily was waiting with a lantern on the bridge and put her arms around her and led her into the Hulk.

Dan being away, I found another boatman, and we pushed out into the river. I stood up in the boat and looked over the waste of ice and snow. Under the leaden sky lay the lifeless Hulk. About the entrance and on the bridge were black dots of figures, standing out in clear relief like crows on the unbroken snow.

As I drew nearer, the dots increased in size and fell into line, the procession slowly creeping along the tottering bridge, crunching the snow under foot. Then I made out little Emily and a neatly-dressed woman heavily veiled.

When the shore was reached, I joined some fishermen who stood about on the beach, uncovering their heads as the coffin passed. An open wagon waited near the propped-up foot-bridge of the Hulk, the horse covered with a black blanket. Two men, carrying the body, crouched down and pushed the box into the wagon. The blanket was then taken from the horse and wrapped over the pine casket.

The woman drew nearer and tenderly smoothed its folds. Then she turned, lifted her veil, and in a low voice thanked the few by-standers for their kindness.

It was the same face I had seen with Emily in the woods,—the same that lay upon his heart the last night I saw him alive.